C000212143

Broomsticks, Walking Sticks and Zimmer Frames

Sue Moorhouse

Ecanus Publishing

Ecanus Publishing
Ramsgate
Kent
United Kingdom

Published by Ecanus Publishing 2013

Sue Moorhouse asserts the moral right to be identified as the author of the work.

All rights reserved. No part of this publication may be reproduced, stored in a retrieval system, or transmitted, in any form or by any means, electronic, mechanical, photocopying, recording or otherwise, without the prior permission of the publisher.

ISBN: 978-0-9574126-5-1

The Fairy Godmother

I hear them talking about me sometimes. They don't do it on purpose, mind. They're kind enough. They just don't know I'm listening.

'Look at her,' they say. 'That little stooped thing, wispy grey hair, trotting around the corridors, confused, never able to settle. You wouldn't believe she had once been the equal of any witch or magician in the kingdom.'

I suppose it's difficult for them to remember that old people were young once. They can't imagine us as we used to be. I don't feel any different in myself, though. I just can't seem to remember things. Forgetful, that's the word — I think.

That woman comes to see me now and again. They call her 'Lady Gertrude' in here. I call her Big Gertie. She brings those two lumps of girls of hers, like great eleph…things. Huge grey things with the ears and the long…Well, anyway, those sort of visitors are enough to make anyone go funny in the head. Oh, they're all sweetness when anyone else is here, but when it's just me they call me the daft old bat. Rude. They only come to make sure I'm still here, safely out of their way, because they're frightened of me. Still frightened of me, even now I'm so decrepit. What a laugh. Well, I don't want to see them, any of them.

Ella comes to visit me every day; my goddaughter. I am always afraid I might not recognise Ella, but I always do. I hope I always do. My memory is erratic. I can't be sure. I would hate not knowing Ella. I looked after her when she was little, after her mother died and before that Gertrude, her stepmother, arrived on the scene.

Today I asked if I could go home with Ella and she cried. I didn't mean to make her cry. She's a kind girl. Too kind for her own good maybe, but you can't help loving her for it.

Ella says I have to stay here, where they can look after me, because I get confused. She says she hasn't got a proper home, either. She says Big Gertie makes her live in the kitchen and do all the work in the house. Too lazy to live, those great lumps of girls are. They never liked Ella, not even when Ella's father was alive. It's not right, having to live in a kitchen.

Not that I want to live here, either. This isn't my home. I lived somewhere else, but I can't quite remember where it was. They keep moving me around, though they say I haven't been anywhere, just this room where they look after me. I don't know. It's a nice room and I have my own furniture. At least they say it's my furniture. I can't say I recognise it.

When that Big Gertie comes, she talks at me. She's like a television set switched on all the time, talking and talking. She goes on and on about a dance some prince is holding; a Christmas ball. She and the two clumping great girls are going. All done up like a dog's dinner, necklaces and… those things you pin on your clothes, them…all over her. Flashy.

My lovely girl Ella looks tired, her hair is greasy and her clothes are dirty from cleaning the ashes out. Her hands are rough and red, too. I wrap them up in the blanket they put over my knees and try to make them comfortable for her. I want her to have a nice dress so she can go to the party. She doesn't know how much it means to me that she comes to visit every day. I'm too old. We shouldn't get so old. I don't want to go though, not until everything is all right for Ella.

'I'll give you some money for a ball gown and a…thing you drive…car, to get you there,' I say.

She doesn't believe me and she is trying to be kind and tactful. 'Don't worry now,' she says. 'It doesn't matter. They'd never let me go, anyway.'

'Now!' I shout. I get up from the chair and I'm angry. I am aware that I'm shouting. It has to be now. It has to be while I remember. Tomorrow I might have forgotten. I will have forgotten.

Then it occurs to me that I haven't any money any more. They confiscated my bag and they look after it for me. That's their story anyhow.

It'll have to be the other way, then.

I haven't done any of *it* for a long time. You never lose the ability, though. It's like riding a…

what do you call it? A bicycle is what I mean – not that I can ride a bicycle any more. I can still make things happen, though. I've made my whole career out of my talent for magic. I was good, that's why the woman Gertrude is frightened of me. I've even done magic in here sometimes. I know the people who look after me are busy, but sometimes, if they don't answer my bell, they just find themselves where I need them and they're not quite sure how. It's unprofessional to use magic for oneself, really, but this time it will be for Ella.

I just look at her and make myself concentrate and suddenly there's a very beautiful girl in my room. Her hair is long and shiny and she is wearing a white, glittery dress, like the sun on snow, and shoes so delicate and sparkling that they look like ice or glass. I know it is Ella because there's her sweet face, but I am confused for a moment. I ask if she is a fairy and we both laugh, I don't know why. She says no, but that I am her fairy godmother and she kisses me.   She is smiling and happy.

'You are going to the ball in a pumpkin,' I tell her.

She looks surprised. It didn't quite come out right. I start to laugh again.

'I didn't mean a pumpkin. I meant one of those cars, luxury cars. That's it a...one of those cars. And a chauffeur.'

There's a mouse, and he lives in the wall of my room. It's one of those big, old houses, you see, this care home. I like mice, anyway. I call him out when I want some company. He'll make a lovely chau…chau…driver. This time I just look at him and concentrate and…

'Look out of the window,' I tell Ella. The view from my window is the front drive, all neat gravel and cut grass lawns.

She gasps. 'Is that for me? It's a white Rolls Royce.'

Not quite the car I meant, but it will do. The mouse looks very handsome too, sitting in the driver's seat in a white peaked cap. I don't know. I suppose he'll be able to drive since I changed him into a driver.

'You must be back by midnight,' I tell Ella. 'I can only keep the spell going while I'm awake and I always drop off at midnight. Old age, I can't help it.'

When I wake in the morning I am tired. I stayed awake very late last night. I can't remember why now. I look at the little mouse, which is running around in the corner of the room, in and out of his hole after the crumbs I give him. There is something I should remember and it was to do with him. I'm almost sure it was.

Big Gertie comes to see me again and she brings those two great ugly daughters of hers. I don't mean ugly faces, which doesn't matter. I mean ugly inside like she is; unkind. She is telling me about the ball the prince gave, on and on she goes. The prince has fallen in love, she says. He is looking for a mysterious girl who appeared and danced with him all night and then ran away. She is watching my reaction, looking suspicious. I don't know why. Mysterious, absconding girls have nothing to do with me.

'Probably didn't want to marry into the royal family. I don't blame her for escaping,' I say.

The girls look at each other and sneer and snigger.

'No, no, dear,' says that woman. She is looking relieved now and using her 'patient' voice. 'The prince has her glass shoe. It fell off when she rushed away. He has given out a proclamation that he will marry whoever the shoe fits.'

'What if she doesn't want to marry him?'

'Don't be so stupid. Everyone wants to marry a prince,' Big Gertie snaps. Her patience becomes exhausted at record speed when she is talking to me. 'We can't stop,' she adds smugly. 'The prince is touring the town with the shoe and we are all going to try it on. My girls may soon be royalty.'

She's just gloating again. Glass shoe. How could you wear a glass shoe? It would break when you walked on it.

Ella comes in later. She kisses me and informs me that she had a wonderful time.

'I'm glad, love. What were you getting up to?'

I ask.

'I went to the ball and I danced with the prince. It was wonderful!' She is smiling and bright-eyed and blushing and she looks beautiful to me even without the glittery dress.

The glittery dress. And suddenly I have remembered everything; the mouse and the pumpkin and everything. And I understand about the lost shoe. I can see it in my mind's eye, white and delicate like glass, like ice.

Ella is smiling dreamily. Love at first sight all round it seems, since he…the whatsit…the prince, is searching the town for her. And here she is, wasting time visiting me when she should be out there, trying on footwear with this besotted prince of hers.

'Take me out,' I say. 'Please. Borrow the thing…I mean the wheelchair, and take me out. I want to see this young man.'

She does — but it takes time, what with telling people where we are going and getting settled in the wheelchair with coats and rugs and all the usual tiresome accoutrements. Good word accoutrements. That came out all right.

There are crowds overflowing the streets when we get out there and everyone is excited. It's like a carnival.

'I don't suppose we will actually see the prince in this crowd,' says Ella sadly. There she is, dirty and half-ragged and friendless, apart from a daft old bat like me. How can she even dream of getting near the prince again?

Well, calling a prince to me can't be much more difficult than calling a mouse. In fact, it's quite similar. I concentrate.

And there he is, a nondescript, nice enough looking lad, embarrassed more than anything because there is that woman, curtseying and showing all her teeth at him and her two daughters are trying to force their great smelly feet into the glass slipper I made for Ella. Dressed up like… well, something big and overdressed they are; all low necks and wobbly flesh and too much of everything bulging out in the street in the middle of the day. They are hopping around and red in the face and effing and blinding with the pain as they crush their toes, trying to cram them into the shoe.

'When you've quite finished, here's someone else wants to try,' I call out and I'm still using the power, so they listen to me for once.

I prod Ella forward, though she tries to shrink away. Doesn't want him to see her like that I suppose. Well, if he's going to marry her there's times when he'll see her looking worse. Even the young look rough first thing in the morning.

The prince comes over. He doesn't recognise her yet. I can see that.

'That's just Ella,' shrieks one of the great ugly girls. 'It can't be her shoe.' They scream with laughter at the idea.

My girl's foot slides neatly into the delicate glass slipper. The prince looks into her eyes, puzzled for a moment, and then a smile spreads over his face like the sun coming up. Suddenly they are dancing again and he is whirling her round and round and she is blazing with happiness.

And I am laughing and laughing and laughing with joy.

There's still great excitement going on all around me. I'm sitting here in my wheelchair. I suppose somebody will take me home eventually.

Not home, I don't mean home. I mean the place where I live now.

Wherever that is.

<u>The Planning Officer</u>

Ms Bacon? I am here on behalf of the Planning Department. I am afraid I have the unpleasant task of giving you notice to vacate this property. You seem shocked Ms Bacon, yet you have consistently failed to respond to our letters concerning your flagrant planning transgressions. This dwelling is an illegal construction, as you have repeatedly been warned. Our records show that you have entered no official appeal against eviction, although you have been given ample opportunity to do so. The Council now requires access to begin demolition work.

What was that, Ms Bacon? Where will you go?

I am afraid that does not fall within my remit. I deal only with planning matters. My advice would be to contact Social Services who have a statutory duty to relieve homelessness. Perhaps a relative could give you temporary accommodation in the meantime? As the representative of the Planning Department my responsibility is to enforce our Green Field Sites regulations. You cannot simply throw up a building wherever you please — even if the building were suitable — which it is not. Building regulations must be adhered to; dwellings must be constructed of approved materials, brick or stone being preferred. Your house may be suitable for a Medieval Life theme park, if you will excuse my little joke, but it is inappropriate for this area or indeed any other area I can think of. I am aware that straw is an ecologically sound insulating material, but you are required to follow proper procedures, Ms Bacon, like everyone else in the country.

Ms Bacon, I'm afraid I must insist that you open the door otherwise I shall have to ask my colleagues to make forcible entry.

Ms Bacon there is really no need for that kind of language. Council Employees are not obliged to put up with abuse of any kind when engaged in carrying out their duties. Your uncooperative attitude will be noted in my report.

*

Mr. Bacon? Mr. Kevin Bacon? Dear me, I do seem to be encountering members of your family under unfortunate circumstances. Oh, your sister is living with you at present is she? Yes, I certainly had the impression that she was bearing a grudge after our last encounter. No, I really don't wish to know what she called me. I am just doing my job, you know, there is no call for personal spite.

I am afraid that I must ask for access to these premises, also. Once again, no application for planning permission has been received. A wooden structure is also a fire risk, and unsuitable for this site. You were notified of our concerns on several occasions. Wooden constructs must comply with certain standards. I refer you to our planning guidelines regulations Pages 56, 57, 93 –104 and 201 onwards.

I am afraid we have no choice but to take enforcement action. Demolition is scheduled for tomorrow morning, so I suggest you remove all personal effects as soon as possible.

No, Mr. Bacon, you will not have the law on me. The Council is acting within its rights and has obtained a Court Order for your immediate eviction from these illegal premises.

*

Oh, my god! Look at this on my schedule for today. It's them again. More bloody Bacons to evict. Why does it always have to be me who deals with them? They live like pigs, the whole clan of them. The three of them have crammed into a one-bedroomed house now. If you can call it a house. I expect the council will have to re-home them, once we winkle them out of there, next to some poor sod whose life they'll make a misery. It's always the way. Problem families shunted around the area, creating trouble wherever they go, chaotic lifestyles subsidised by the taxpayer. You've just got to look at them; small, scruffy, unwashed, stubbly hair all over their chins. And that's just the sister.

And no, I don't want my remarks put on record. That was my own private scream of rage, thank you. Thirty-five years I've been doing this job. Retirement coming up and does it get any easier? Does it, hell. Some days I ought to be wearing a flak jacket. You wouldn't believe what I've been called over the years. Nazi is the least of it. All I am doing is carrying out the Council's instructions. I don't necessarily always like it.

However, in this case, it will be a positive pleasure.

Ladies and Gentlemen of the planning office, I give you fair warning that my blood is up. If I have any nonsense from those Bacons, I will not be answerable for the consequences. My killer instinct is roused. I shall go straight for the throat. I'll have them for breakfast.

*

Mr. Hamish Bacon, I presume? Yes Sir, I am well aware that this house is bricks and mortar and has always stood here. However, it was originally a bus shelter. You have completely rebuilt and extended it. I know that you have applied for retrospective planning permission, using the appropriate form. I was there when you submitted your application, wrapped around the brick. In fact, I narrowly escaped serious injury. May I draw your attention to the fact that a number of conditions were specified before any planning application could be considered? None of these conditions were discharged before you commenced work on this building and therefore your application has been invalidated. Once again I must inform you that the Council has no choice but to take enforcement action against you.

No, Mr. Bacon, your human rights are not being infringed. In any case the term hardly applies to your family, factually speaking. I'm afraid we have no intention of waiting while you appeal to the EU. I must request you to unbarricade your door and leave peacefully. We are council employees and have every right to enforce access to these premises.

*

Bloody hell, lads, what do you mean you can't break the door down? You've been trying for an hour already. It's reinforced? Well, you've got a bulldozer haven't you? Start it up and let rip. Oh you can't, eh? Not living in Gaza, aren't we? Well, we'll see about that. They're not getting away with it, I tell you. They're pigs, pigs! I'll get in through the roof and open that door. Get the ladder. No, I bloody well don't want to be careful at my time of life. I'll kill them, the lot of them! I won't stand for them sitting there in their filthy sty, laughing at me. Don't you tell me to calm down. I'm not huffing and puffing and even if I were it would be my business. And I don't have high blood pressure thank you so very much.

This is the famous last stand of B. B. Woolf, Esq., Senior Planning Officer.

Now hold that bloody ladder still.

This will be easy. I can see right down the chimney. There's room for Santa Claus down there, never mind me. Come down and stop being an idiot? Of course I'm not coming down, you bunch of pinko-liberal, animal rights sympathisers.

Here we go.

What's happening? What are they doing down there?

Aaaaarrrrh!

Snow White

My dears, this time my regular blog will be a little different. I want to set the record straight before...well, you'll see.

I know that there are dreadful, hurtful rumours circulating. Rumours about me. I notice strange looks and whispers when I am out lunching with friends. I don't believe that I am being oversensitive. There seem to be fewer friends now. My calls are not returned.

Murder. It's such an ugly word. Surely no-one who knows me, or has followed my blog, could believe that I was capable of such a thing?

People will say such dreadful things. Gossip flies around. I've been accused of being violently jealous. Me! As if I would take that characterless little girl so seriously. As for ordering anyone to kill her, it's absolutely absurd. It's sheer melodrama. Why ever should I do such a thing? A woman in my position?

It's a silly story she's made up. Do you know she once accused me of trying to suffocate her by lacing up her corset too tight? Who on earth wears corsets in this day and age? Totally unfashionable. That, in itself, proves what nonsense all this is. It was just a bodice, part of a ridiculous teenage outfit she was wearing. She asked me to help her with it. It was black, of course. Don't teenagers just love black? It was supposed to lace up tightly. Indecent on a young girl, I felt. I like a low-cut neck myself, but I wear clothes that are a little more sophisticated.

So you see how foolish the rumours are. But people are fickle, of course. When you have a social position like mine, it's important to choose your friends carefully. There's so much envy and spite around.

Let me tell you something. In the end we are all alone. The only thing you can always trust is what you see in your mirror.

'Mirror, mirror on the wall, who is the fairest of them all?' I ask, every morning of my life.

'You, lady,' it tells me.

And that is how it ought to be.

Glamour is what I have, or so my late husband always told me. It's a great gift. Of course, my husband has been dead for many years, but I was much younger than him, almost a different generation. My face and body have always been my fortune. I look after them and they look after me.

Those of you who follow my blog will know that I am generous with my fashion advice. I adore clothes. Don't we all? Match your colours, and accessorise with scarves and jewellery, that's my style tip. Real jewellery, not imitations — so cheap, so nasty. I know that many people feel uneasy about wearing fur these days, but I would always recommend the real thing. Expensive clothes have a better cut altogether. Always look for the right label. Good quality is so important, isn't it?

But this blog must be a little different from my usual fashion chat. My dears, I'm sorry to bore you with my troubles, but these rumours have distressed me.

The relationship between stepmother and stepdaughter is always problematic, of course. It could all have been so different if that wretched girl had accepted my guidance. She was just impossible. Always in jeans and T- shirts. No idea how to dress, and wouldn't be told.

She was a pretty little thing when she was small. She had black, black hair, quite natural and very white skin. Snow White her father called her. A nickname, rather silly. She was my bridesmaid when I married him. Everyone said how sweet she looked. Well, I tried, heaven knows. I used to dress her in little outfits to match mine, but she was always running about or fidgeting and getting dirty. It simply wouldn't do. Then, when she was a young teenager it was all sulks and pouts and the terrible clothes they wear; leggings and silly little skirts and black this, that and the other. Ridiculous. She had acne, too. Not a problem I've ever had, let me assure you.

'Mirror, mirror on the wall, who is the fairest of them all?'

'You, lady,' my mirror says, and I know I'm

as lovely as ever. I'm a little more mature in appearance but all the more attractive for it. I've kept my looks. Some of my old acquaintances have just let themselves go, but not me. Make-up is so important. It's simply a matter of touching up the few grey hairs that peep through and doing a little work on the face and neck. There, as good as new. You hear such alarmist reports about facelifts and even good old Botox, but you only have to look at me to see what can be achieved.

Little Snow White was quite pretty as she grew up. A slip of a thing she was, slim and pale, but with that long black hair.

You could see people admired her. But I haven't an envious bone in my body, as anyone who knows me will tell you. I always knew I was the more sophisticated and better dressed. I had my mirror to assure me of that.

I was surprised when my mirror first noticed Snow White. After all it never had before. I wasn't upset though, not for a moment.

'Lady, you are fair it's true,' my mirror told me,

'But Snow White is fairer far than you.'

Such a ridiculous thought. That scruffy child! No, I wasn't in the least troubled. Why should I be? I can still turn heads myself, let me tell you.

'Darling,' a friend said to me over coffee the other day, 'you're so svelte, and your posture is wonderful. You move so gracefully. You're always the last word in elegance.'

So kind. It's lovely to be told.

As for not caring about the girl, I was distraught when she ran away from home. It took me weeks to find out where she was, and I worried constantly. Whatever anyone tells you, I had sleepless nights.

And then to find her living in a household of circus rejects. Not that it surprised me. She always did adopt unsuitable friends. But a young girl living with seven men, however small they are. It's bizarre. Almost obscene.

It would have been quite wrong of me not to visit her. I had to be sure she was safe. I know my duty, however tiresome the girl was. Everything I did was for her own good. To be honest with you, I was quite distressed to see her looking so unkempt, her hands all red and work-roughened from cleaning that scruffy little cottage. The long, dark hair was greasy and tangled. I left her one of my own combs, purely out of the goodness of my heart. Poisoned? Rubbish! Someone in my position does not poison people. Why should I want to harm her, annoying though she was?

And as for the next allegation, all I can say is what nonsense. Apples are good for you. An apple a day keeps the doctor away. I ate some myself, and anyhow, if she'd eaten poison she wouldn't have recovered when the piece of apple fell out of her mouth. More likely she choked herself. She always was a greedy girl. She'll never keep her figure as I've kept mine. She'll be fat before she's

22

forty.

In a way, it's a pity that the young king came along and disturbed everything. She looked so lovely, perfect but pale and lifeless, as she lay there in the glass coffin her little friends bought for her. Sweet. But the young man couldn't just leave well enough alone, he had to wake her from her trance and insist on marrying her. Now she'll grow old, just like everyone else.

And none of us want to grow old do we? Lose our looks? Turn into something ugly and wrinkled?

'Lady you are fair it's true,' says the mirror on my wall.

'Yet the young queen is fairer a thousand times than you!'

That wretched girl. She haunts me. She's so… young. How can I be expected to bear it? Hearing that every day. Why should I?

But I mustn't get angry, however much I'm provoked. It's the surest way to cause ugly lines around the mouth and eyes. One must be gracious. A gracious lady, that's how I mean to be remembered. Through my blog, I've made sure that no-one misunderstands what I'm about to do. There's no question of any wrongdoing on my part. I've simply made a decision.

You see this is goodbye, my dears.

I've smashed the mirror into a thousand fragments. Seven years bad luck, they say. I hope it falls on her. I shan't be here to feel it. I have a long, sharp piece of mirror glass in my hand. Now, while I'm still blogging, I shall open my veins. The blood will flow away and I'll lie here, as white as snow and beautiful as her, forever.

It Gets my Goat

Some snotty-nosed young girl come into my flat the other day and told me I was racist.

'Listen, darlin,' 'I said. 'You don't get me that way. I'm not prejudiced; I hate everyone. I hate the Scots and their bloody Flower of Scotland - that was bloody centuries ago, Jock! I hate the Irish, and the Welsh, gabbling away in some language only six people speak. I hate them Caribbeans and their rap and their street talk. They want to speak the Queen's English. Yeah, and I hate the royal family, load of useless parasites. I hate Scousers and Geordies and Asians and Chinese food and curry, and them women what go about with their 'eads in bags. I hate travellers 'cos they don't pay no taxes, and I hate them EU buggers coming here and taking our jobs, and I hate lazy kids hanging around instead of getting on with a decent day's work. I hate bankers and rich gits and footballers and celebrities and clever buggers and people goin' on about God, and I hate the bloody BNP, load of morons. Oh, yeah, and I hate them noisy kids in the flat above mine. You know what I hate most?' I finished off. 'I hate social workers and stupid little tarts coming here and telling me what I should be doing.'

That told her.

Cheeky little baggage. I can look after myself with no interference from no-one. She said my flat was a health hazard. My business, that is. What's the use of cleaning? After a bit it don't look any dirtier. The whole building's a slum, any road. The lifts don't work and kids graffiti them and pee in them. There's gangs hanging around with drugs and knives. Here she is, worried because my flat's a bit grubby and I'm not politically correct. She wants to sort out some of the real problems. Kids, mainly. Noisy little buggers, think they own the place — especially the ones that live above me, jumping around on them rickety-rackety floors.

A bit of peace, that's all I ask. Fat chance with them upstairs crashing around over me head. There's three bloody kids living up there and no-one to keep them in order. The mother works all hours, leaving them kids running wild and playing the goat. Music, if you can call it music, blasting away. All I hear is thump, thump, thump and me whole flat shaking with it.

I like me own space and me privacy. Not much hope of that, mind. Take the other day. I'd carried a chair out, so I could sit in the sun on the walkway outside me front door. Not a bad view from there. I can see the bridge over the river. I don't mind a bit of fresh air. I can have a fag and a good cough and a spit up to clear me chest. So, there I was, sitting out, minding me own business, when one of them kids from upstairs comes trip-trapping along, ruining the peace, wanting to get by.

He was a scrawny-looking little runt, just about climbing over me legs to get past.

'Here you, bugger off out of it,' I said. 'You're not coming by here.'

'You don't own the walkway,' he said, the cheeky little scrote. 'The lift's bust again. I gotta come this way to get downstairs.'

'That's your hard luck,' I said. 'I'm sitting here, and I'm not shifting.'

He give me that hard-eyed stare that kids do. He was wearing one of them hoodies too. What did you get for Christmas, sonny? A little rioter's outfit?

'You can get yourself back to your own flat,' I told him. 'And keep the noise down.'

'But I need to get by,' he bleated, putting the tears on, trying to get round me that way. 'We got no food in and I gotta go down the shop.'

'I'll bloody have you for my dinner if you try and push past me,' I said.

'I'll tell my social worker about you,' he threatened. 'And I'll tell me brother, Billy. He'll be down. He'll sort you out!'

'Oh, go on then. On your bike,' I said and I let him shove past. You got to be careful with kids. You can get yourself in trouble if you give them a bit of a slap. My old man used his big leather belt on me and nobody ever said a word to him. Never did me any harm. He used to knock me mum about too. The youth of today don't know they're born. They need a nanny, some of them.

Half an hour later, would you believe it, another of them kids comes along. A bit older this one was, about thirteen, maybe. He was as skinny as the first one and all done up like a dog's dinner with his underpants sticking out the top of his jeans. What do they think they look like?

'Your flat don't half stink and you do an all,' he pointed out, charming little bleeder. Then he started to push past me legs, nearly treading on me with his great, clumsy hooves in them posh trainers.

I gave him a bit of kick. 'Oh no, you don't, Billy Boy,' I said.

'How'd you know my name?' he asked, suspicious like, glaring at me and stamping his feet a bit.

'Your brother told me.'

'Well, if he went down, why can't I?'

''Cos I live here and I don't like the look of you,' I said. 'And I'm bigger and stronger and nastier than you.'

'Yeah, you're not wrong there. My mum says you're a troll, like them tweeters that leave horrible messages on tribute websites and that. Always got something bad to say about everyone, you have.'

'Yer, that's right,' I said and I give him a grin showing all me teeth. Not what they were, me teeth, 'cos I've broken a few and they've gone a bit orange, but I've still got most of them.

He took a couple of steps back. 'That's 'orrible! You leave me alone, or my older brother'll see to you.' He was bleating as much as the little one now, not even phoney tough.

'Bring him on,' I said.

I'd had enough of talking to the likes of him by then, so I jerked me head at the stairs. 'Go on. Get out of it.'

That kid went by me at a run, like he thought I'd got two heads and was going to bite him any second. I like to see 'em scared. I haven't had so much fun for years. I looked over me balcony and saw him down below. He was sitting on the steps, talking on his mobile, yelling, it looked like. Telling his mates and his brother how brave he'd been and what a horrible old bastard I was, probably. You could just bet that number three of them kids would be on his way down here in a bit. What a laugh!

Five minutes later I heard him coming down the stairs, too, thundering down more like. He was a lot older, this one. Blimey! Look at the size of him. He had a beard starting and he was built like a brick shithouse.

'I want a word with you,' he said in this deep, gruff voice.

Before I knew what he was doing, he'd grabbed me and head-butted me right back into my flat.

Good job I've got a bolt and chain on me door. I tell you, I got that door locked so fast you'd think I'd never heard of arthritis.

That bastard banged on it for a good five minutes before he went off.

Kids today, terrorising defenceless old people!

It gets my goat.

Scandal at the Towers

Sexual intercourse began

In nineteen sixty-three (which was rather late for me)

Between the end of the Chatterley ban

And the Beatles' first LP.

Up to then there'd only been

A sort of bargaining,

A wrangle for the ring,

A shame that started at sixteen

And spread to everything.

Philip Larkin

The newspaper headlines were simply ghastly.

'Scandal at Elite Girls' Boarding School.'

'Matron Questioned by Police about Accident at Girls' Public School.'

Only the local paper was decently restrained: 'Tragic Fall at Well Respected School,' it said.

And that was the simple truth, Enid Batt thought firmly. It was all a frightful accident.

Nothing like this had ever happened to Miss Batt before. She comforted herself with the thought that generations of old girls of The Towers School remembered her fondly. Good old Batty, they called her. She had kept them on the straight and narrow and guarded them from the wicked world outside.

She knew who she blamed. First there was the new headmistress and her human biology lessons. In Miss Batt's opinion, it was better not to mention S E X at all. It put ideas into innocent girls' heads.

Then there was the new gardener. He was far too young and personable to be employed in a girls' school. She had noticed the girls watching him out of the tower windows. One warm day she had even had to send someone running out to tell him to put his shirt back on. Working half-naked in front of all her girls! The very idea!

And, of course, there was Punzi Applegarth. Punzi. What a ridiculous nickname for a child. What were the parents thinking of? She was a little madam, that one! Seventeen, going on twenty-seven. Far too sophisticated for her age, or thought she was. A silly girl. She would come to a bad end if Miss Batt couldn't knock some sense into her.

Every day was a struggle, with Punzi in the school.

'Come along girls, look lively. Clean sheets today,' cried Miss Batt crashing open the doors of Dorm 16 in her usual hearty manner.

'Oh, Batty!'

'Hurry up, now,' she urged, chivvying the more lackadaisical. 'Top sheet to the bottom, bottom sheet to the wash and a clean new top sheet on, neatly tucked in. Rapunzel Applegarth, what have you been doing with your bed? The sheets in this dormitory look as if they have all been tied in knots.' She gave a brisk tug at a recalcitrant bottom sheet, and roared on energetically. 'There's no excuse for slovenly bed-making. If a thing's worth doing at all it's worth doing properly.'

'It's not worth doing at all,' commented Punzi Applegarth, and all the girls laughed.

There seemed to be sniggers everywhere Miss Batt went. Girls simply weren't what they had been in her young day.

'I say, girls. Less noise, please. Turn that appalling racket down. It's not music, it's just caterwauling. Yeah, yeah, yeah, what on earth does that mean?' Miss Batt snorted. 'Yes, Punzi, I'm sure I am square, but I won't have pictures stuck up on the walls either, making marks on the paintwork. I don't know why you all want to gaze at those sissy long-haired youths.'

'It's like being locked up in prison,' she heard Punzi say, as she passed the dorm door next day. 'or a convent. Old Batty is absolutely obsessed with sex.'

There were peals of laughter from Punzi's chums.

The cheek of it. Miss Batt stomped heavily into the room, a dignified figure, she felt, in her tweed skirt and sensible lace-ups. 'I can assure you,' she asserted sternly, 'that any interest I have in...hanky

33

panky...is entirely in the cause of safeguarding you young girls, while you're in my care. A matron's job is a great responsibility. My word it is. You must remember girls, that young men will not respect you if they think you have loose morals.'

They all laughed, would you believe it? Quite above themselves, and needing to be firmly squashed. She was not going to tolerate them ragging her.

'I think you are very rude,' she told them severely.

'Who cares?' Punzi flashed back at her.

'Don't care shall be made to care,' Miss Batt retorted darkly. 'Don't care shall be hanged.'

Rather a vindictive saying, Miss Batt had to admit, on reflection. Perhaps a little extreme. In any case, thinking about hanging simply sent her mind off at a tangent, reminding her of the ropes she had found in Room 16 at the beginning of term. Rapunzel Applegarth and her chums had explained that they were for practising gym. She had removed them, naturally. A dormitory was not the place for physical education. However, she approved of her girls using up their energies in healthy sports. Except swimming, of course. That meant taking off far too many clothes.

Room 16 was a thorn in Miss Batt's flesh. It seemed to be a magnet for all the slackers in the sixth form. She found that ghastly book in Room 16. She couldn't prove it belonged to Punzi

Applegarth, but she had her suspicions. Lady Chatterley, indeed! A member of the upper classes behaving like that. Miss Batt thoroughly agreed with the prosecuting lawyer at the obscenity trial. She certainly didn't think that any modest-minded woman should read such a book. She had confiscated it, naturally, and noticed that the pages were turned over to mark certain excerpts, which she had read with absolute disgust.

'I'm sure I left that book out of sight in my cupboard,' Punzi retorted slyly, when reprimanded. 'I hope no-one's been rummaging in my drawers and interfering with my chest.' She smirked at her friends, and shrieks of laughter pursued Miss Batt, as she slammed the door and strode away down the corridor.

That girl was a disruptive influence.

Then there were the strange plaits of hair. The girls did spend an inordinate amount of their lives doing each other's hair, of course. Hair styles these days seemed to be either loose and untidy, or in those ridiculous beehives. Miss Batt much preferred the bunches and severe plaits of yesteryear. Nevertheless, the two long, coarse plaits of false hair she found in Room 16 puzzled her.

'Oh, they're for a fancy dress party we're all going to in the holidays,' Punzi told her innocently. 'You can wind them round and round your head to make a really elaborate hairstyle.'

She demonstrated, posing in front of the mirror.

Miss Batt breathed a sigh of relief. What the girls did in the hols was up to their parents. If they really had to meet boys, she much preferred them doing it then, when they were not her responsibility.

Then, came the night of the ghastly accident.

Every evening Miss Batt made a last patrol of the dormitories at eleven. On that particular night she heard giggling and whispering in Room 16. She crept closer, trying not to tread too heavily or breathe too hard, and listened at the door.

There was more suspicious giggling and muffled shrieking. Those girls had no business to be out of bed and making a noise at that time of night.

'Rapunzel, Rapunzel,' a voice called from somewhere outside. 'Hurry up and let down the bloody hair, will you? I can't wait all night. Someone will see me.'

Good Lord! It was a man's voice.

There they were when she entered Room 16, Punzi and her chums, dangling those long plaits of false hair out of the window. Miss Batt was across the room in two strides, thrusting her head out to see what was happening. Great Heavens! The man was halfway up the wall, climbing the plaits of hair that the girls had tied to the window frame. It was that gardener. The blighter was trying to gain access to her girls' bedrooms.

The horror of it. The scales fell from Miss Batt's

eyes; knotted sheets, ropes and now the false plaits of hair. This must have been going on all term. Immorality! Sexual intercourse! Possible pregnancy! Right under her nose.

Rage filled her.

She could not remember clearly what happened next. In retrospect though, she was quite sure that she had behaved calmly, a dignified figure of authority. She was doing her duty, protecting her girls from the evil influences of MEN. Whatever the girls claimed to the police and their parents, she was certain she had not burst alarmingly into the room, pushed them aside and deliberately dislodged the plait the youth was clinging on to. Absolutely not. He must have simply panicked when he saw her furious face, and fallen. It was all his own fault.

It was unfortunate that he had landed on the crazy paving, and the stone flower troughs. He had broken rather a lot of bones. Nearly all of them, in fact. Of course it was very regrettable. However, she was sure he would be almost as good as new in time, once he got out of hospital, and out of plaster, and all the fuss had all died down.

In any case, it was all the doing of that wicked, immoral girl, Rapunzel Applegarth.

She certainly wouldn't be coming back to The Towers next term.

Head to Head

They never did find my body.

No one even noticed I'd gone, if you ask me.

There were no articles in the newspaper reporting the sad passing of a respected local witch, deeply mourned by family and friends. There was not even a short paragraph at the bottom of page five saying: 'Old witch's decomposed corpse found. She had been dead for months and partially eaten by cats.'

In any case, there are two things wrong with that last scenario. Number one, something quite different happened to my body. Number two, I didn't have any cats. I can't understand why anyone would believe that a cat is a good familiar for a witch. The wretched creatures have minds of their own. There's no doing anything with them. Then there's the question of litter trays.

There wouldn't even have been a police enquiry into my death, except for the food poisoning scare. You remember I mentioned that something quite different happened to my body? Well, I don't think they cooked me properly. There was never any trouble when I was making the pies and sausages. No salmonella in my produce, I can tell you. Poor standards of hygiene, that was the problem. It all comes from ignorance. Kids today think they know it all, but they don't. It makes you wonder if they are even taught Domestic Science in schools now. They probably kept their raw meat next to their cooked meat – make that their raw me next to their cooked me.

You might wonder how I am chatting to you now, seeing that I've been horribly murdered. I shall explain. Have you heard the fairy tale where the talking horse goes on giving the princess good advice even after it's been decapitated and had its head nailed to a stable door? Well, what happened to me is similar, except that I'm considerably more intelligent than a horse and was capable of speech in the first place. That makes it more realistic, doesn't it?

The heads are always a problem; I've found the same myself. They are bulky and hard to process. You can't just leave them lying around. It upsets people and that is inconsiderate.

The little buggers who finished me off were, naturally, trying to hide the evidence of their crime. They were very cool and calm about it; I must give them credit for that. They managed to get rid of the rest of me, but my head — the centre of my being, the seat of my soul — is just stuck on a shelf like a museum exhibit, shrivelling slightly and going green. They didn't even put my glasses back on, which makes it difficult to keep an eye on things.

It all started with the teenagers hanging around my house, pestering the life out of me. It's not as if I live on a rough housing estate. My home is a traditional witch's gingerbread cottage. I suppose it is a bit like living in a sweet shop, but as for luring the kids here, I couldn't keep them away. If I didn't watch them they'd eat me out of house and home; bites out of the walls and snacking on the window ledges. Bad for their teeth, all that sugar, but what do they care?

Come to think of it that's another thing that's difficult to get rid of, the teeth.

Anyway, in my opinion it's a disgrace the way modern kids behave. Feral, they are these days. Strangle a hoodie, that's my motto. Playing football, and damaging my flowers - lovely Deadly Nightshade and Laburnum I've got - and making a din. I was always having to go out and yell at them:

'Get out of here, you little buggers!'

I'd curse them too. 'You'll be old yourselves one day. I hope somebody comes and makes your life a misery. I hope you get arthritis. And piles.' Good curse, that one. Most of it is bound to come true in time and that's good for the street cred.

I could probably plead self-defence for what happened to those teenagers. You're always hearing about old people being terrorised by yobs; gangs of them, running riot, stealing and violent. If those young louts had stayed at home and done their school work they would have been perfectly safe from me. I suppose, strictly speaking, I should have a legal disclaimer over my door. Something like: 'The resident witch cannot be held responsible for any injury to trespassers on her property. Anyone vandalising her home and annoying the hell out of her does so at his, or her, own risk.'

Think of me as a kind of Victorian Cautionary Tale witch. They had a sensible attitude to the young, Victorians. Badly behaved children got eaten by bears or had their fingers chopped off for biting their nails. I feel that I combine the two penalties in quite an imaginative way.

I know the modern consensus is that witches were wise women and healers, who were misunderstood in superstitious times. Either that or they were poor, lonely, demented old souls who looked funny and talked to themselves and were persecuted by ignorant religious maniacs. Well, there's a lot of truth in that, I'm not denying it. However, you should just think of me as the other kind of witch. If I had a job description tag pinned onto my blood-stained, black clothes, it would say: 'Evil Old Hag.'

I have wandered from the point a little here. Let us return to those teenagers. They made a nuisance of themselves, swearing and shouting and breaking things. The insults I had to put up with. I know I've got warts. Witches are supposed to have warts. When I was a girl I'd have got a clip round the ear for being cheeky to my elders and betters. No good telling the parents these days. They're worse than the kids. They'd be round here shouting at me if I complained about their obnoxious offspring. No parental responsibility. They don't even seem too bothered when the kids go missing.

I do tend to take the noisiest, nastiest ones, I suppose.

Don't get me wrong, I like kids. I couldn't eat a whole one though, ha ha.

Well, actually, to be honest, I could. Not all at once of course. You know what they say — waste not, want not. They make lovely sausages, eighty per cent meat with herbs and seasoning, not too much bread in them. I used my mother's old mincer, since you ask, and her big washing copper. Boil everything up well, until it's falling off the bone, then through the mincer. Add a bit of onion and so on. My own recipe. There you are, black pudding and pies too, to sell at the farmers' market. No-one ever got ill from my home cooking, let me tell you.

Before you say anything, I'm not a cannibal. Cannibals live on islands in the Pacific and paddle around in canoes, half naked. I don't hold with that, not in this climate. I'd catch my death.

Which reminds me, my death was what I was telling you about. It just so happened that the next kids who knocked on my door were rather different. They were a little younger, smaller but tenderer you might say, and quite nicely spoken and polite — to start with at least — a very different kettle of fish. There was a boy and a girl together.

The other gang of louts probably sent them to me as a joke. They were looking for a place to stay. They said their stepmother had thrown them out of the house and they had nowhere to go. They would have to sleep on the streets if I didn't help them. They had no coats, just thin track suits, the cheap, shiny ones. Neglected, if you ask me. They were almost like the barefoot kiddies back when I was a girl, nowt but skin and stick. I don't think they got enough to eat. They'd chewed through half the porch before I even got to the door.

'Come in, my dears,' I said. 'We'll soon get you nicely fattened up. Plenty more food inside.'

Well, if I'd known what was going to happen I would have sent them on their way, but it's easy to be wise after the event. The event in this case being me getting cooked and decapitated by the little brutes. At the time, I felt almost sorry for them. You might say that I just took them in out of the goodness of my heart. Put it another way, if the mice walk into the cat's mouth that's their bad luck and it doesn't reflect on the moral character of the cat.

Well, of course, they wanted to leave the next morning but I couldn't have that. I had to lock the boy up in my crow cage. Proper wire that cage is, nothing you could eat your way out of. As I said, I've never liked cats as familiars. Crows have a bit of an eyeball fixation and a tendency to crap everywhere, but they are very good at clearing up bits and pieces that can't go into the pies. The problem was that the boy never seemed to get any fatter. The girl, Gretel, she was called, made herself quite useful about the place. Bright little thing, I was actually thinking of taking her on as an apprentice. We were getting on quite nicely until I found out what they were up to. She was giving the boy old bones to stick out of the cage instead of his arms so I thought he was still skinny. She was trying to take advantage of an old woman with bad eyesight. Ageist, I call it.

Well, that was it. I wasn't waiting any longer. I couldn't trust them could I? I had the Aga door open ready and I told the girl to have a look in and see if it was hot enough. She turned round and said she wasn't sure and I'd better have a look myself. In retrospect, I can't think how I was fooled so easily. Too innocent and trusting I suppose. I was muttering to myself a bit, along the lines of 'incompetent kids can't do anything right,' and then I bent down to look in.

Do you know what the little bugger did? She pushed me in.

It was roasting in there, I can tell you.

I must admit, I'm proud of that girl. Gives me a lump in my throat, or it would if I had a throat. She'd have made a fine witch. It's not every young lass that feels comfortable pushing old women into ovens.

They could have got away with killing me if they'd just made it look like an accident, or they could, quite legitimately, have claimed it was self - defence but the two of them got ambitious, like all amateur criminals. They decided to dispose of the evidence Sweeney Todd fashion. Of course, the pie-making equipment was readily available in my cottage. I like to think that perhaps it was my example they were following, and that I had some formative influence on their little minds. I don't want to get involved in the whole Nature versus Nurture debate, but it would be nice to think that I'd made a difference.

Well, as I said before, no-one would have found out if it hadn't been for the outbreak of food poisoning. When the hygiene inspectors arrived they discovered several ingredients they were not expecting. Things were still stuck in my mincer. I could have warned those kids. You don't put the fingernails in, let alone the toenails, I would have told them. Toenails are worse than bits of apple core in a pie.

I've no hard feelings towards the youngsters. I must be mellowing with age, though I doubt if there was ever any likelihood of my turning into a sweet little old lady.

Anyway, the kids are too young to be held criminally responsible, apparently. They'll probably just be given counselling for post-traumatic stress. They'll have to move away from the area, of course. People can be very squeamish.

So, there we are. I've enjoyed our little tete a

tete.

Now remember, kiddies, don't talk to strangers. Especially if they offer you sweets.

The Musicians

The original Grimm fairy tale was called The Musicians of Bremen — a cat, a dog, a donkey and a cockerel, all past their prime of life and now useless on their respective farms, are discarded by their owners. Together they leave home to travel to the city of Bremen and make music. On the way they encounter some robbers

*

Titch, the whippet, lay with her nose under her garden gate. Through the gaps in the ironwork she saw Mick, the big, aggressive, ginger cat from next door, jump stiffly down into the road. He gave Titch a nod and ambled over to speak to her.

'I'm off,' he growled. 'You won't see me round here again. I heard them say they were going to tie a brick round my neck and drop me in the pond. Useless old moggie hasn't caught a mouse for months, they said. Charming. That's what you get for a lifetime of service.' His tail swished angrily.

Titch whined sympathetically.

'You want to watch it yourself,' the cat went on. 'You're not as young as you were, either. I haven't seen you chasing around much lately.'

'It's my arthritis,' Titch admitted. 'I can't run as

47

well these days.'

'That's not good news for an ex-racing whippet, is it?' Mick said. 'You'll be for the one-way trip to the vet any day now. If you're lucky,' he added darkly.

'Do you really think so?' asked Titch, alarmed.

The cat yawned, showing horrible yellow teeth. 'Stands to reason, doesn't it? Come along with me, if you like.'

Titch's thin tail wagged anxiously a couple of times. 'But where will you go? What are you going to do?'

'I'm going to be a travelling musician,' the cat announced. He opened his mouth and emitted an ear-splitting yowl.

Titch found herself howling along, involuntarily.

'Nice vocals,' said the cat. 'We could make it big together. A group always has more chance of success than a single artiste.'

Titch hesitated. It wasn't that she was species-ist; in fact the whole dog and cat antipathy was something she deeply deplored. It was just that Mick made her nervous, with his battered fighter's face and scarred fur. There was something about him that made her hackles rise.

She was a home-loving dog, and running away was a big step. She hadn't much choice though, had she? If Mick was right, it was either take to the road and become a rolling stone or face a terminal trip to the vet.

With one last frightened backwards glance, she slipped out through the hole in the hedge and joined him.

A little further down the road they came to the field where Dave D the donkey lived. He was standing with his head hanging over the gate, looking muddy and depressed.

Titch went to touch noses with him. She was fond of Dave, with his velvety coat, soft brown eyes and long eyelashes, even though he was not the brightest quadruped in the paddock.

'What's the matter?' she asked.

'I've been put out to grass,' said the donkey gloomily. 'No use any more because I'm getting too long in the tooth. Not that there is much grass in here,' he added, 'and only a tree for shelter, summer or winter. No-one ever comes to see me or groom me anymore, just boys who throw stones at me. It's a lonely sort of life.'

'Why not come with us? We're travelling musicians now,' Titch told him, as cheerfully as she could manage. 'I'm going to do vocals.'

'And I'm vocals and guitar,' the cat interrupted. He was sitting near the gate with all the claws extended on his front paw, surveying them with a satisfied expression on his face. 'Look at them fingerpicking claws,' he said, flexing the paw.

Dave D turned and beat out a thunderous

rhythm on the field gate with both back hooves. 'Percussion,' he said.

Mick eyed the piece of string which stopped the gate from swinging open. 'That shouldn't be much of a problem,' he said. 'Not to an expert in breaking and entering like me.'

A little further along the road they came upon Beaky the cockerel. He was standing on the verge, screeching at the top of his voice.

'Chicken pie,' he screamed. 'They've brought in a new, younger cockerel and they are going to make me into chicken pie!'

'You'll be a bit stringy at your age,' commented Dave D, who was, frankly, a bit dim and tended to say the first thing that came into his head.

'I doubt whether worrying if he'll make a delicious chicken pie is something that will have Beaky spinning in his grave,' commented Mick sarcastically. 'Spinning in his gravy,' he amended after a moment's thought.

The cockerel shrieked louder than ever.

'I think you would make another excellent vocalist,' said Titch soothingly. 'Why don't you come along with us? All of us have been thrown on the scrap heap after years of hard work, just because we are old.'

'We have pulled our weight all our lives,' agreed the donkey. 'Titch was well known in the racing world, and then there was your rodent control business, Mick, and me with my career in haulage…'

'Donkey work!' said Mick cattily.

'That's right,' agreed Dave D, who probably thought irony was something to do with horseshoes. 'Then there was Beaky's career,' he went on, 'in the…er…'

'The sex industry,' said the cock smugly.

'He's a gigolo,' remarked Mick. He surveyed the floppy comb on the cock's head and the dishevelled feathers. 'Was a gigolo. Anyway, the point is that after giving them a lifetime of service they've treated us like dirt. We don't owe them a thing. They won't care for us in our old age, so it's make our own way in the world or starve. Brothers and sisters, let's hit the road.'

Beaky recovered his vanity quite quickly once they were a few miles down the road, away from the disdainful hens in his old chicken run. He preened his feathers and strutted along, showing off what was left of his good looks. He was very much the rock star when it came to matters of appearance.

Titch wondered if that was quite enough to ensure the group's success. 'Shouldn't we try rehearsing together?' She suggested diffidently.

Everyone seemed to agree. Even Mick didn't argue.

They found a quiet place in the shadows of

an old cliff, where there was no-one to overhear them. The rehearsal went splendidly, as far as they could tell. The birds flew off quite early in the performance but, as Mick pointed out, they didn't need an audience at this stage in their careers.

'I think that went quite well,' said Titch timidly.

'It was amazing,' crowed Beaky. 'Now we need a proper name for the band. How about the Yardbirds?'

'That's a typically egotistical suggestion. You're the only yardbird in the group,' Mick growled. 'It should be The Animals.'

The donkey gave them a puzzled look. 'But we've got names already,' he said. 'I'm Dave D...'

'You're dozy,' interrupted Mick rudely.

'... and the rest of you are Beaky, Mick and Titch,' went on the donkey, ignoring him.

As the excitement of the rehearsal drained away, a thoughtful silence fell. The sun was going down and the evening chill was beginning. The musicians were facing the prospect of their first night on the road.

'About now', said Mick yearningly. 'We should be checking into our luxury hotel, with roadies to carry our equipment and a manager to take care of all the arrangements for us.'

Titch was beginning to be anxious again. She was cold, all the others had thicker coats than hers, and she missed her home comforts. There was no hotel. Even if there had been, she was sure that Mick would have clawed the curtains and Beaky would have pecked the mirror and by the time they had got Dave D in as well, they would have trashed the place. She whimpered a little.

'Don't whine,' Mick told her unsympathetically.

'I'm hungry,' said Dave D. He sucked up a few dead leaves off the ground.

'We could peck around for worms and beetles,' suggested Beaky.

'Or we could have fresh chicken,' snarled Mick. 'None of the rest of us eat insects!'

Tempers began to fray. It had been a long day for them. They began to feel moody and a little blue. Beaky fluffed his feathers, tossed his head and flew off to perch on a high branch of the hollies above them. The others settled down to make the best of it. Titch and Mick curled up uncomfortably on the sandy shore and Dave D shut his eyes, rested one leg and philosophically fell asleep.

'I can see a light,' Beaky crowed excitedly after a while. 'It's quite close by. It could be a farmhouse. How about sending out a couple of searchers to see if it's safe?'

'Let's all check it out together,' said Dave D, opening both eyes. 'Farmhouses have hay.'

'And cream,' agreed Mick with a touch of a purr in his voice.

When the four walkers finally arrived at the

farm, drawn by the warm, homely-looking lights, they found it a strange sort of place.

'I can't smell any trace of cows or sheep,' Titch pointed out, lifting her long nose and sniffing. 'There's just an odd sweetish smell that seems to be coming from all that weed in those greenhouses.'

Beaky flew up and perched on the window sill, looking into the lighted room.

'The good news is that there's a table spread with lots of food,' he reported. 'The bad news is that two men are sitting at it. They don't look like very nice people.'

'There's no such thing as nice humans, sonny,' snarled Mick. 'Now then, lads, and bitch — all right, all right, only joking — we need to get ourselves in there. Let's give them some music, just vocals should do it and I don't think we need worry too much about harmonising. I'd say a bit of dissonance is the key to this particular door.'

Titch scrambled up onto Dave D's hairy back and let Mick claw his way up on top of her. She fought down her urge to bite him and, instead, enjoyed watching his expression when Beaky perched on his head.

'One, two three…' she barked. 'Altogether now.'

'Ee ow, woo woo, cock a doo, meroow, eeow, woo woo, meroow.'

As the noise reverberated around the farmhouse,

the door slammed open and two figures sprinted away, screaming, into the darkness.

'Thank you choir, and rest,' said Mick with sardonic satisfaction.

Sure enough, just as Beaky had said, there was an excellent meal laid out on the table. They fell on it like ravening beasts.

'They'll be back, you know,' Titch said a little later, when anxiety had had time to reassert itself. 'They'll be looking for us. Probably as soon as it gets light in the morning.'

'Well, at least we can get a good night's sleep,' said Dave D.

'Ooh, yes,' said Titch. 'I need a night on a comfortable bed. I haven't got the kinks out of my spine after lying down under the Hollies back there.'

'I'll keep watch,' growled Mick. 'Excuse my cynicism but I wouldn't trust any of you lot to stay awake.'

Mick, himself, must have dozed off. He woke with a shock to hear stealthy human footsteps right inside the house. He opened his eyes cautiously and saw someone creeping closer. Unexpectedly, the footsteps came rapidly towards him and the next moment the intruder had tried to stick an unlit cigarette in his eye. Mick's reaction was outrage; a whirling cyclone of unhygienic old teeth, claws, halitosis and spitting.

The screaming intruder recoiled across the room. 'I thought it was the fire that I was lighting my fag at. I thought it was glowing coals!' he shrieked. He staggered across the room and tripped over Titch, who instinctively stood up just as he was trying to step over her. She bit him hard, as high up the leg as she could reach. The taste was bad but it was wonderfully therapeutic.

'Don't stab me. Don't stab me again. Please. I'll get out. I'll get out.'

A moment later there were thuds and yells outside as Dave D finally caught up with events and joined in the brawl with both back hooves. Beaky shrieked rhythmically to add to the confusion.

'Police sirens!' screamed the intruder.

After a while, there was silence. A very thoughtful silence.

'I don't think I can stand much more of this,' said Titch timidly. 'I think I'm just too old to be a member of a group.'

'I know what you mean,' agreed Beaky. 'Maybe we should call ourselves the Pacemakers. That's what I'm going to need if I get any more shocks like that.'

'Jerry and the Pacemakers,' said Dave D. 'My bladder's not up to all this excitement, either.'

They turned to look at Mick, who so far hadn't said a word. His eyes were half shut and he was purring softly to himself.

'I've had a better idea,' he said. 'I think I know what that odd-smelling weed in the greenhouses is. It's called cannabis and humans can't keep off it. It's a bit like catnip.' The glint in the old cat's slitted, yellow eyes was evil now. 'Forget about music,' he snarled. 'We'll become drug dealers instead.'

The Pied Piper

'Talking of rats. I had a pet one once. Nice little thing it was.'

Silence greeted Peter's comment. He felt embarrassment settling on the room. It was a 'Let's humour Dad', 'Don't upset Granddad' kind of silence.

Oh dear. Perhaps he shouldn't have mentioned rats. He smiled at his family as they sat politely round the table.

'Well, lovely to see you all. I'll just be in my… shed.'

He stood up and moved towards the door, still smiling vaguely.

'Granddad, can I come?' That was Jamie, his grandson, seven now. He followed Peter out of the door and jogged beside him across the garden, talking all the time. Jamie was excitable, hyperactive and a sufferer from chronic verbal diarrhoea. Peter adored him.

'I'd love a pet rat too, but you know what Mum thinks about rats. She's like Aaaagh!' Jamie shrieked.

Peter nodded. 'I was just thinking about the rats…' his voice trailed off absently.

'You are lucky, Granddad. Having this workshop and everything,' said Jamie enviously as they reached the shed.

Peter's shed was a little more high tech than the usual. It was more a sound studio; aerials, computers, switches to flip and buttons to press for flashing dials and high frequency noises. They liked fiddling with things, kids, Peter thought, watching Jamie. To tell the truth, so did he. Who was it that claimed to have spent his life just picking up pebbles on the seashore? Some famous person. Probably famous enough to avoid being patronised by idiots. Or did that happen to everyone? Well, at least in his workshop Peter was his own man and he could do what he was good at. The world didn't have to approve.

According to Peter's ex-wife the shed was his equivalent of a snail's shell. If anyone wanted to carry the analogy on, they would say that out in the real world he was soft and defenceless, like a slug; not a thought that appealed to him.

He still had bitter memories of sitting on his lone chair facing that semicircle of overbearing, condescending men and women. They had behaved rather as he imagined MI6 would when interrogating a suspected terrorist. How did they have the nerve to speak to anyone as they had spoken to him?

He hadn't deliberately caused trouble. He had simply been discussing points arising from his research. Points that should have been aired and tested, not just ignored as inconvenient. The trouble was that the people in charge of companies were not scientists.

The browbeating and the aggressive accusations of disloyalty and incompetence had been an eye-opener for him.

'Are you telling us that you know better than the other scientists working for us, Dr Stanhope?'

'No, no! I just...

'How is it that no-one else has suggested that mobile phone signals have a detrimental affect on bees, Dr. Stanhope?'

'Well, my doctorate was on the effect of sound and microwave radiation on living creatures. I feel qualified to make the connection.'

An explosion of contempt had shattered his self-defence. 'Are you totally naïve? Don't you realise the damage you will do to the company by rocking the boat with this kind of wild theory?'

'I just want to see proper experimental analysis,' he had protested. 'Mobile phones seem to upset bees and other creatures, but it might not even be the electromagnetic radiation from the microwave range of the phone that is affecting them, you see. And if it is, there might be a way of dampening the radiation...'

'Do you really think that that is the impression that your interviews with the media have given?' one of his inquisitors had interrupted.

That had been his big mistake, speaking to the

papers; sadly journalists were not scientists either. The reporter who had asked to interview him had seemed rational enough, but the headlines had been dramatic and inaccurate. They had brought up old fears about mobile phones destroying human brain cells and lowering sperm count. They had quoted Einstein: 'If bees disappeared from the face of the earth, man would have no longer than four years to live.'

It was bad science, and his bosses had left him in no doubt that it was bad business practice too.

He had left the company, been asked to leave. He had taken early retirement, officially due to stress-related illness, though in his opinion his illness was caused by sheer disgust at the human race; sickness, literally.

Still, there were compensations. He could get by on his pension. He still couldn't quite believe that he never had to go to work again. He woke up with such a feeling of relief each morning. Even knowing he was considered some kind of useless failure by most people couldn't spoil it. Respect would be nice, of course, for his family as well as for himself. They had been very good really, very protective of him, but it was not easy to accept that he was someone who needed that protection.

He had been working on his current project all summer. It would be economically useful, and thus an achievement that other people might value, and even pay for. It had to do with the rats. They were everywhere this year. They were breeding in the sewers, popping up out of toilets and getting into people's houses. A plague, the local paper called them. It was quite a clever headline really – rats, plague – but, as ever, not conducive to reassuring the paper's readers. The rats seemed to like the wet spring they'd had. They had had three litters of young that year, and rat poison was having no effect at all. Apart from the odd one or two that had the decency to act poisoned, the rats seemed to quite like it. The town was crawling with them. The pest control officers were run off their feet. Judging by the letters in the paper, rate payers were getting stroppy, frankly, about the council's ineffectualness. Not surprising really. A rat is quite a pretty little thing on its own, but thousands of them can be a bit of a nightmare.

Higher frequency waves seemed to affect animals most. There were plenty of rats breeding under Peter's shed for him to observe. He had been tinkering for months, and had found a signal they reacted strongly to. When he played it they popped up, as if someone was promising them cheese and bacon and a place in rat paradise.

It was just a matter of using a field-effect transmitter now.

He hadn't discussed it with the family. He didn't want to worry or upset them, but he was looking forward to demonstrating his little brainchild.

'Want to be my assistant Jamie?'

'Yeah, Granddad!'

The town council was desperate, which was just as well, as Peter suspected he would be no sort of salesman.

'We'll try anything once, Dr Stanhope,' the chairman of the council said. Peter recognised the expression. He knew exactly what the man was thinking: 'Dr Stanhope, eccentric, to put it politely, got a lot of wild ideas, had some kind of breakdown didn't he? Shame really, clever man of course. Well, if we let him try, at least it shows we are making an effort. People can blame him instead of the council when it doesn't work.'

Peter supposed cynicism was another useful kind of snail shell.

However, if he was going to do this he was going to do it properly.

First there had to be the arming of the champion.

His ex-wife had always moaned because he kept all the junk that had meant something to him over the years. There were spare room drawers and wardrobes full of old clothes, smelling of damp and mould. One was an old sixties outfit, a Carnaby Street uniform — red, with epaulettes and gold lacing, just like the ones on the Sergeant Pepper album cover.

His daughter was gobsmacked, frankly.

'You're actually going out in public in that,

Dad?'

'It's brilliant, Granddad,' Jamie said. 'But why are you wearing it now?'

'Because…' Peter said. Because the sixties meant things like love and peace, and not doing what you were told by the leaders of the land, he thought. Because there had been those gentle, happy people at Woodstock, and the imagery of bombers turning into butterflies. Because he had been young then, and clever, and dreaming of something better.

It would be too difficult to explain that feeling to Jamie.

Peter sang it instead, or warbled it, slightly out of tune. 'Because the world is round, it turns me onnn. Because the sky is blue, it makes me cryyy. Because the wind is high, it blows my miiind,' he sang.

Sergeant Pepper, what an album, he thought, and grinned at the laughing Jamie. 'I may be living in a world of tangerine trees and marmalade skies, and I'm certainly Sixty Four, but I'm still hoping it's Getting Better.'

'Cool, Granddad.'

'And don't follow leaders and watch your parking meters,' Peter added as an afterthought.

As he walked through the shopping precinct, next morning, with the recording device in his backpack transmitting its seductive rat sound, people either ignored him or laughed at the show. Jamie was with him, dancing around. It was like busking, like an entertainment, and that suited him fine.

Then the laughter stopped, because following them down the street came thousands and thousands of rats. A writhing sea of rats spread from one side of the shopping arcade to the other, claws clicking as they ran, scaly tails wormlike behind them. Shoppers were screaming, as rats scrambled over their feet. Panicking people dashed into shops and up steps, or climbed onto seats and walls, as the horde of rats poured single-mindedly on, pursuing Peter.

Right out of the town they went in procession, with Peter leading in his Sergeant Pepper finery and the rats scampering happily behind him like an unlovely kindergarten outing. Out there in the countryside, miles away from any human habitation, surely a rat could be a rat without bothering anyone? 'There's a place for us, somewhere a place for us,' Peter sang, hopefully, as they left the town behind them.

And when Peter returned, with just Jamie, beaming, beside him, the streets were lined with cheering crowds. Even his family and their friends were looking at him differently. For once he was the man.

'You'll have to understand, Dr Stanhope. The

council is facing big cuts to our budget this year. Much as we'd like to purchase your clever device, I'm afraid there are just no funds for it. And, of course, we don't have the rat problem now so, unfortunately, our rate payers would not really benefit from further outlay,' said the chairman of the council.

So. No money, then. That shouldn't have been entirely unexpected, Peter supposed.

He could, of course, try to get his research into this project published in a science journal. He probably should have taken out a patent too. Someone, somewhere, would most likely profit from his idea.

It all just made him feel tired. What was the point?

And Peter felt an unusual anger. A whole lifetime of frustration, and lack of appreciation, was coming to a head. All the promises and dreams that had been wasted.

It wasn't hard to change the note of his music. Human beings are animals too, after all. And soon, not just Jamie, but half the kids in the town had started to hang around, fascinated, near his workshop.

When Peter strode down the street again, dressed in the clothes of his youth, every child in the town was following him, laughing and yelling. Parents snatched up the little ones, which was for the best, but the rest followed him happily out of town.

'Don't put ideas into Jamie's head,' his daughter had once said, in a kind but firm sort of way. 'He needs to be practical. To succeed in life.'

But what else should you have in your head if not ideas? What else should children have in their heads?

'Where are we going Granddad?' asked Jamie.

'I don't know, Jamie,' said Peter, shrugging as he walked.

The smile on his face was gentle, but very, very strange.

The Grandmother

You worry more when you're a grandmother. When I think of the things I used to let my kids do, it makes my hair stand on end. It's only natural to get more cautious as you get older, more aware of all the terrible things that might happen

That was why I bought my little granddaughter that bright red coat, with a cosy little hood to keep her ears warm when she's riding her bike. She loved it and I thought it would stand out well on the dark winter mornings. She was my first grandchild and that's always special. Grandma's little girl, she is. You always wonder whether you will feel the same about the grandchildren as about your own, but you do. As soon as they are born, you love them and want to protect them.

It's the children I worry about. I'm not nervous for myself; not even now after all that happened. I may be getting on a bit but I'm not a helpless old dear yet. I've never been a poor weak woman either. People are funny about feminism, either shouting about it or sneering at it. It is just common sense, I say. You have to take care of yourself as best you can, not wait around and hope some man will do it for you. Of course, I'm on my own now and not as young as I was. I still go to yoga, but it used to be judo and those self-defence classes where you poke people in the eye and stamp down on their ankle bones. Not that I would, I don't think, but you never know what you might have to do in a crisis. These days, I'd probably do my hip in, or rupture a varicose vein, if I tried anything too physical.

When the nightmare does come true it's always a shock, isn't it? I know my cottage is a bit isolated, but I've always preferred to think of it as off the beaten track, and that's often safer. I've never even bothered to lock my door, except at night. I love being out here in the peace and quiet of the woods. Just having the trees around me makes me happy; the green in spring, the birds and squirrels and the autumn colours, and then the shape of them in the winter, black and sculptured against the sky. The people around here are mainly forestry workers and they're friendly enough.

I suppose, after what happened, I'll have to think about moving into sheltered accommodation, but sheltered housing is all in towns and you don't get the view and the peace and quiet. Still, I can't expect the family to trail out here to my cottage, when I can't manage for myself. There's my granddaughter too. She's at that age where she wants to go out on her own, just old enough for her mother to let her. It is a worry her coming out here on her own. When she does any cooking with her mother, she often fills up a little basket for me and brings it round, bless her. She makes lovely cakes and her pastry is better than mine, even when it's been dropped and stepped on a few times. Not that I make pastry nowadays. I buy it at the supermarket. It saves all the mess.

But that's beside the point. It's what happened that matters.

It was just lucky that I was out of sight at the time, in the bedroom, making my bed. I heard the door slam and someone burst in, making an angry snarling noise, and I caught a glimpse of this enormous hairy man in my kitchen. He was wearing a hoodie, and that's always a bad sign, judging by what you hear on the news. You could see his ears sticking out under the hood, though, and as for his face, well, poor soul, the nose on him and the hairiness.

I didn't like the look of him one bit, and I didn't like the noise he was making, either. It was more animal than human. I wasn't going to pop out and ask him what he was doing there! I slipped straight behind the door, and then under the bed. Amazing what you can do when you're scared. Although whether I'd ever get up again was a different matter.

Tramps, they used to call them. I suppose it's the homeless now, though there's homeless through bad luck, and there's just plain trouble. I thought he'd probably steal some food, or a few bits and pieces, and be on his way. I wasn't going to argue, not the size he was.

Well, I was wrong. He came straight into the bedroom. I thought he must have heard me and my heart was in my mouth, I can tell you, but no, the first thing he did was get into my bed. Cheek! I'd have to change the sheets straight off. I could smell him and it nearly made me sick. I wasn't sure I'd fancy sleeping in those sheets again, even after they'd been washed a dozen times. I lay under the bed watching his reflection in my full-length mirror. He pulled the bedclothes right up to his chin and sat there with his hood still up. He looked like someone in an old-fashioned night-cap. I nearly laughed aloud, half hysterical. That would have torn it.

The next minute there was nothing to laugh at all, because I heard a banging on the door and a voice calling, 'Grandma. It's me!' and in she came, my little granddaughter, with her bag of cakes. I heard her footsteps, as she looked in the other room for me, then there she was at the bedroom door, wearing that nice coat I'd bought her, with the little red hood still up.

Well, she wasn't stupid or myopic and she could see it wasn't me in the bed.

'Ooh, Grandma, what big ears you've got,' she said, the cheeky little madam.

'All the better to hear you with, my dear,' said the hoodie man, in a silly, falsetto old lady voice. It was all quavery. Not a bit like me.

'Ooh, Grandma, what a big hairy nose you've got.'

'All the better to smell you with, my dear.' He'd

got a nerve talking about smell.

Well, my granddaughter knows her fairy stories and she wasn't going to do the next bit was she? She shot out of the bedroom and ran for it. The hairy man leapt out of bed to go after her, and I had to stop him, so I hit him as hard as I could on the ankle with the white china potty that I keep under the bed for emergencies. Well, it was an emergency all right. It's a very painful place to be hit, the ankle bone. He almost fell over, and he was swearing like you wouldn't believe. He reached under the bed for me, still swearing and furious. He was hurting my arm, so I bit him. I bit him so hard that my top set of dentures stuck in his hand and I heard them clatter on the floor, as he shook them off.

I was half under the bed and half out, hanging on to him to keep him there, while my little girl got away. I don't know what would have happened next, but she came bursting back in with help. She had found a forestry van just down the road and there was one of the tree surgeons with her, holding a big chainsaw. It's surprisingly easy to make a citizen's arrest, when you have a chainsaw in your hand.

Well, he rang the police on his mobile and my granddaughter crouched down to peer under the bed. Very pale, she looked.

'Are you all right, Grandma?'

I was shaking a bit, you can imagine, but you've

got to put a good face on things, haven't you? I didn't want the little lass getting nightmares.

'I'm fine, love,' I said. 'But can you get me out from under this bed?'

We managed it in the end, and stood there, puffing a bit. I reached down and picked up my top set of dentures, sucked them back in and wriggled them around to get comfortable. I'd be shaky later, but just then, I felt wonderful.

My little lass grinned at me. 'Ooh, Grandma, what big teeth you've got.'

'All the better to bite the big, bad wolves with, my dear!' I said.

The Intruder

When Mr. and Mrs. Brown returned from their weekend break they found their house in a shambles. It was every parent's nightmare. They had left their teenage son at home on his own for the first time. He hadn't, he couldn't have… thrown a party?

Mrs. Brown felt a chill of dismay. Surely their son would never do such a thing? He had been such an adorable baby, and although he was going through the shambling adolescent phase, he would grow out of it, wouldn't he? The matted hair and filthy claws of fingernails, and the piercings in his poor nose, and growling and grunting when they spoke to him wouldn't last forever. On the other hand, they were older parents, she and Daddy. Perhaps they were out of touch and just hadn't realised the sort of behaviour he might be capable of.

Their kitchen was in a terrible state. There were half-eaten bowls of food all over the table and the mess had overflowed and been trodden into the floor all through the house.

'Pooh. What a stink,' complained Mr. Brown.

When they checked the sitting-room, they found broken furniture. One of Mrs. Brown's favourite chairs was completely splintered.

Heaven knows what had been going on in there.

74

Had their son been drinking? Or taking drugs? Fighting? You could never tell, could you? Perhaps there was a more innocent explanation. He could have invited a few friends round — no harm in that — and then some older ones might have come along and forced their way inside. Gate-crashers. Nasty types.

She wanted to find an excuse for him, but on the other hand how would gate-crashers find the house? He surely wouldn't have been stupid enough to arrange a party on the Internet? You heard of that happening, and she wouldn't put it past him. Sometimes she didn't know what was going on in his head.

They had been in her bedroom, too. The bed was rumpled. Someone had been lying on it, without even taking their shoes off, and had made black marks on the satin bedspread.

'Oh,' she wailed. 'They've been in our bedroom. It's as if our home's not our own anymore.'

'We'll have to just grin and bear it,' said her husband consolingly. 'I've checked under the mattress and our money's still there, so that's one good thing.'

'But, Ted, it's the idea of a stranger lying on our bed. I feel as if an intruder might be hiding and spying on me. It makes all the hair at the back of my neck prickle.' It was all too much. She could have wept.

Her husband gave her a consoling hug.

'Where is that irresponsible young cub, anyway?' he muttered. 'We leave him to look after the house for two days and this happens.'

She could tell that he was getting upset, too — or getting angry, which was his way of being upset. Oh dear, having him like a bear with a sore head was not going to calm the situation when their son did return.

It was half an hour before the culprit slouched in and then he nodded to them, as if nothing was wrong at all. 'Oh, you're back,' he said vaguely.

'No, we're still away. That's why I'm standing right in front of you, shouting at you,' his father snarled. 'What's been going on here?'

'Dunno,' their son gaped around vacantly at all the mess. 'What's happened?'

'That's what we want to know. We came back and found a mess.'

'Well, it wasn't like this when I went out this morning. I left everything clean for you coming home. I knew you'd get like, grizzly, if it wasn't neat and tidy.'

Mrs. Brown could see her husband's blood-pressure rising.

'Well, it's not tidy now. Either you've been having friends in and it's got out of hand, or you forgot to lock up when you went out this morning and we've had intruders,' he roared. 'You don't seem to care.'

Their annoying offspring shrugged. 'I thought I locked the door. Maybe I forgot. Sorry and all that. Is there anything missing?'

Mrs. Brown had not considered that actual burglars might be responsible. It didn't bear thinking about.

'Whoever it was has obviously gone,' her husband growled irritably, turning to their son. 'The only room we haven't checked is your pit of a bedroom.'

The teenager barred the way, protective of his private space. 'That's my room. You keep out. I'll check it.'

A moment later, they heard his cry of shock.

'What is it? Have you've found a burglar?'

'It's not a burglar. It's a girl,' reported Mr. Brown, pushing his way into the room after his son. He didn't sound all that relieved about it. 'What I want to know is what she's doing in your bed, bold as brass, my lad.'

'Fancy bringing your girlfriends in here without a word to us,' Mrs. Brown protested. 'You know we would be happy to have your friends to stay, but in the spare room, not in bed with you. Not at your age.'

'Get a grip, Mum,' he growled rudely. 'I've never seen her before. I've no idea who she is, or how she got here.'

The girl in his bed was quite bare. Unfortunately,

however, not their kind of bear. There was no excuse for it. Mixed species relationships were just wrong. Think of the children...cubs... What would the neighbours say? Mrs. Brown could hear them now, rabbiting on, and badgering her for information.

At that very moment, the wretched human woke up. She stretched and yawned as if she'd had a good night's rest, looking quite at home. Then, she saw the Browns and screamed. She was out of that bed and off like a hare. They heard the footsteps rushing down the stairs and away out of the front door.

'Well, if that's not guilt, what is?' Mr. Brown asked severely.

'Look, Mum, Dad, I swear I've never seen her before. I don't have a clue who she is, or what she was doing here,' protested their son.

'A likely story. I suppose some completely unknown golden-haired girl just happened to wander into our house, eat our porridge, break our chair, try out all the beds and then climb in yours and fall asleep, did she?'

'Well, yeah,' he said.

'That's a fairy story if I ever heard one,' Mrs. Brown said in a voice of utter disillusionment.

The Princess and the Pea

The idea came to Dorothy and me as we were making our way down the corridor, on our way to dinner. There was a sudden blast of a horn behind us, loud enough to give anyone heart failure, and a voice shouting, 'Look out! I'm coming through.' We flattened ourselves against the wall and Loretta came hurtling by on her mobility scooter. It's not even as if we are supposed to have them inside the care home. Somebody could get mown down. Mind you, with the kind of lack of consideration for innocent bystanders she displays, it wouldn't surprise me if she attached knives to the wheels like Boudicca.

'I wonder if she really is a princess,' said Dorothy, as we got our Zimmers pointing the right way again and generally sorted ourselves out.

Officially Loretta is just a plain 'Missis', like the rest of us, but she always claims that her proper title is princess. 'I am distantly related to the exiled King of Ruritania,' she told us. Actually, it probably wasn't Ruritania. I turned my hearing aid off when she started monologing about it, so I'm not sure. The horn on her mobility scooter plays the first four notes of their national anthem, anyway.

Don't get me wrong, I like royalty, in moderation, and I've nothing against people having delusions.

My friend Elsie, in the room across from mine, thinks it's 1930. As my husband used to say, 'Everyone's strange save thee and me…and thee's a little strange.'

What I can't do with is Loretta expecting special treatment. You should have seen her furniture when she moved in; a Regency commode and even her bed had those little curtains round it. In this place we're more into plastic sheets on your anti-bed-sore mattress. And she's so demanding. You wouldn't believe it. The carers are so busy dealing with her tantrums that the rest of us could collapse in the corridor and they'd only have time to step over us on their way to her room.

Anyway, I was thinking over Dorothy's question about whether Loretta was really a princess. 'We should test her and see,' I suggested. 'You know the old story where the prince hid a dried pea under ten mattresses and the real princess was the one who complained that she'd had an uncomfortable night because she could feel the pea?'

'The version I heard, the princess had to pee through ten mattresses,' said Dorothy. She can be crude at times. Still, bodily functions, or lack of them do tend to be our chief conversational topic here.

'We ought to try it,' I said. 'It would be a laugh.'

'It wouldn't be safe to put ten mattresses on her bed,' said Dorothy. 'We'd need the hoist to get her in and she'd probably break her hip if she fell out.'

'We could try her with a dried pea under her normal mattress,' I suggested.

'My daughter's coming to take me shopping tomorrow. I could buy a packet of dried peas,' said Dorothy speculatively.

Well, we were cackling like a couple of idiots by the time we got to the dining room. All through lunch we kept catching each other's eye and giggling.

Don't get the idea that I'm subversive in any way. I'm no trouble to anyone, ask any of the carers. You need a laugh in here, though. It's nice enough, but the days are very long. You can't get about much and there are none of the little jobs that used to fill up the time.

We're not an unfriendly bunch. Generally we rub along together and look after each other, apart from the odd spat. Loretta was a nasty bully from the word go, though. I heard her, telling a visitor that she had to sit with two incontinent old hags at lunchtime. That was poor old Louie and Joyce.

I think 'prize bitch' is the term I'm groping for here, if you'll excuse the language.

Anyway, I'd almost forgotten about the dried pea idea by the next day. It was what happened at lunchtime that started it all off again.

We'd all just sat down at our respective tables to eat when Loretta started up.

'This soup is disgusting,' she yodelled.

'What kind is it?' Ron asked. It's difficult to tell at times.

'I think it's pea,' said Loretta.

'Don't be silly,' said Dorothy, quick as a flash. 'It's soup.'

Do you know, I think even Loretta smiled slightly at that one, in a frosty sort of way.

When Dorothy went out shopping with her daughter that afternoon she came back with a packet of dried peas and brought them round to my room to show me, a conspiratorial expression on her face.

'I'll slip a pea under her mattress, ready for tonight,' she said.

'Go on then,' I dared her.

It would be quite easy for Dorothy to do. She's as sharp as a tack in most ways, but she does tend to forget where she is. No-one turns a hair when Dorothy wanders into their room.

She reported back about half an hour later, while I was getting ready for bed.

'Mission accomplished,' she said, saluting smartly.

Well, none of us gets up very early in the morning, but the management like us all to come down for dinner at midday, so we knew everyone would be there. We'd told a few friends what we had done and we were waiting with bated breath to see what the Princess would say.

She made her grand entrance and condescended to sit, and we all settled down.

'Did you sleep well?' Dorothy asked her innocently.

There was a silence, broken only by the squeaking of hearing aids, as everyone craned to hear the answer.

'I didn't sleep a wink,' said the Princess dramatically.

'Ooh, what a shame. Why not?' asked Dorothy, mugging like mad.

'I had terrible indigestion all night. It must have been that dreadful pea soup for luncheon yesterday.'

Dorothy looked at me and I looked at her. Neither of us could think of a thing to say.

To this day we still can't work it out. Does that mean she really is a princess?

Or not…?

<u>The Christening</u>

I was dreaming about my daughter. It was one of those dreams that you have just before you wake, where you can recall every detail before it fades.

In my dream, I relived my ridiculous disappointment when we found out that our baby was a girl. I was in my fifties and I knew that this might be our only child. I so wanted a boy. You can't admit that, though, can you? Not in this day and age.

Naturally, I was moved by the miracle of birth, messy though it was. I helped my wife with her breathing and told her when to push, and so on. She wasn't very appreciative, but I realise that she had a lot to contend with; all that blood and screaming and sweating. Even allowing for female exaggeration, it looked a pretty uncomfortable business.

I didn't like holding the baby for the first few weeks. I kept wondering if it was supposed to look like that, or whether those jerky movements and unfocused eyes meant there was something wrong with it. It was only when she first smiled at me that I really knew that she was my little girl. Daddy's little princess.

I helped as much as I could, of course. I changed

a nappy several times, got quite a dab hand at it. She was a very good baby. By the time she was three months old my wife was only up once in the night with her. At that age, of course, we had to have her christened. The family expected it of us.

If only we had just ignored those expectations.

That christening was a nightmare. You wouldn't believe the carry-on we had, poring over lists of friends and relatives. The ramifications were endless. So-and-so had to be invited because we wanted her sister to come and we couldn't ask one without the other. All that kind of thing. We were knee-deep in magazines about table decorations and christening cakes and there were menus from caterers piled on every flat surface.

My job was to book the church and the vicar, and organise the marquee for the lawn. None of that took me more than an hour or two. Then I just had to fetch out the tailcoat I'd had for the wedding. Even the baby's outfit caused more trouble than mine, since both sides of the family had traditional christening outfits they wanted her to wear.

Things went wrong right from the beginning of that christening. Firstly, the vicar didn't seem to have any idea about babies. He had four babies to christen that day, but he kept us all hanging about, while he spouted his religious guff for half an hour, or more. Well, of course the babies had had enough by then. They were all screaming, and all the mothers were getting frazzled, and the godparents were thanking heavens that they could hand the noisy little buggers back after the ceremony.

Our little girl had whole sheaves of godmothers. It was the old can't-ask-one-without-the-other syndrome. We were up to our necks in them. It can be a bit of a cynical business, choosing godparents, deciding which ones are likely to stick around and take an interest, which ones can afford good presents, and which ones have power and influence and will be able to pull a few strings for the kid in later life. Their religious beliefs are secondary, to be honest. I'm not sure any of our lot were very Christian. In fact some of them definitely weren't — magical powers have always run in our family. The poor vicar would have been horrified, if we had told him.

It was one of those days. That's all I can say. It was hurling it down with rain when we came out of the church, so it was a case of finding umbrellas, rushing to cars and trying to keep the baby dry. She was dry outside, anyway. The nappy was another matter by then. That caused another hiatus. Projectile pooing! It was half way up the windows in the car and all the pretty, lacy white christening clothes were a mess.

By the time the baby was changed and fed, the guests were queuing up outside the marquee wanting to be greeted and allowed to get at the food and drink. The rain had eased off by then, fortunately. There are always the folk who want to clasp your hand and reminisce for hours, when you just want to get them into the tent, so that you can say hallo to the next lot.

We finally got everyone into the damn marquee and there was a general scrimmage for seats, and people were getting in a huff because they weren't sitting at the table they thought they ought to be. The only person who was calm was my little girl. She sat there on her little chair and beamed at the confusion as if it was all arranged for her entertainment, bless her.

There was a big pile of christening presents on one of the side tables. Beautifully wrapped, most of them were; all white and silver with long ribbons decorating them and meaningful little messages, so we would be sure to know who to be grateful to. There was a gold bracelet that you could add charms to, with the words: 'May your little one grow in beauty with the years.' One of my aunts, who used to be a head mistress, had given her the complete works of Shakespeare, with a message wishing her intelligence and a good school career. My wife's cousin, who's a concert pianist, gave her Mozart for Babies, and hoped she would inherit the musical talent. She was going to be quite a girl with all these magical good wishes, I could see that.

Then it happened. The curse of 'Don't-forget-Cousin-Mildred—or-she'll-be-upset'struck. Inevitably, someone had been left out. If you are going to offend someone you want to make sure it's a shy, quiet family member, who won't like to make a fuss. We got it disastrously wrong there. We forgot Evil Edith, as she's known in the family. There was no chance that she was going to stay quietly at home and put up with being insulted. She's a nasty old bat, but, unfortunately, a magically powerful one. There she was, striding down the marquee, all dressed in black, with steam coming out of her ears and the most malevolent expression on her face that I've ever seen on a living creature.

'Your baby will never live to grow up. When she's sixteen, she will prick her finger on a sewing machine, and die!'

She didn't say it loudly, more spat it out, but everyone in the marquee heard it all the same. You could have cut the horrified silence with a knife. Then the whispers started. As she stalked out, everyone backed away as if she was a poisonous spider, not even wanting to let her shadow touch them.

My poor little baby just sat there and smiled sweetly. I could have wept. I wanted to snatch her up and run out with her, to protect her forever. The emotion was pure caveman. No one was going to harm my child. I'd kill them first.

Then the last of our godmothers spoke up. 'I cannot undo such a powerful curse,' she said, 'but I can lessen the effect. This lovely baby will not die. She will sleep for a hundred years, and all of you with her.'

That was the end of the christening from hell.

Well, you can imagine, that curse hung over us for the whole of my little girl's childhood. We made the most of every moment, feeling that time was precious. Such fun we had, games and holidays at the seaside, ponies, guinea pigs, trips to the cinema, books and parties.

Of course, the first thing I did was to ban every sewing machine from the house. When our daughter was little, we never let her out of our sight, but it grew more difficult as she became a teenager.

'Give me space, Dad,' she used to shriek, and she'd lock herself in her bedroom.

She was never nasty with it, though, never a brat or a whiner. She was so pretty and we always knew she loved us really, even through all the teenage rebellion.

The trouble is that children are always attracted by the forbidden. It's natural, I suppose. If we had insisted she did nothing but sew all through her childhood, she would have refused to touch a needle. Because we had banned it, she wanted to learn to sew and knit and crochet and do all those girly things that my wife says she so resented being forced into as a child.

To this day I don't know how that sewing machine got into the house. I heard my wife shriek and I ran upstairs, feeling my heart thumping fit to burst with the sudden exertion. I was not far off seventy by then. I'd kept myself in shape, but even so, I was not as fit as I had been; a bit heavier, a bit slower in reaction time. If only I had been faster. I've brooded over it, again and again, imagining that I got there just in time, instead of just too late.

'Don't touch it!' I heard my wife cry.

Oh Mum, it's just a sewing machine. What do you think is going to happen? I can't exactly impale myself on the needle, can I?' I heard my little girl say.

And then, I fell asleep, instantly, like having an anaesthetic. I wasn't even aware I had been asleep, until just now, when I woke up and remembered all my dreams.

It felt no different from waking in the morning. Could we really have slept for a hundred years? I looked around, bleary-eyed, and wished someone would bring me a cup of tea. There was no-one to do it, though. Everyone seemed to be in the same state. e had been asleep on the floor and old bones and joints were protesting about it, vehemently. I thought I'd never be able to straighten up again. My wife looked like some kind of mad woman, with hair down to her waist. My own beard would have thatched a cottage, and I had long hair too, like some damn hippie.

I stared at the dust and cobwebs and the dark, filthy windows. Half the light was blocked out by trees that had grown into forest. I tried to adjust to

90

what had happened to us. A hundred years have passed, I thought again. It didn't seem possible.

I'd hardly had time to even begin to come to terms with it, when my daughter was there, smiling, and as pretty as ever, looking not a day older.

'Mum, Dad,' she cried, flushed with excitement, her eyes sparkling. She pulled a young man forward, clinging onto his hand and beaming shyly up into his face. 'This is Prince Jamie. He woke me with a kiss.'

There he was, some drippy-looking, spotty youth. Creeping about, kissing my little girl in her bedroom.

'Get your hands off her,' I roared.

'Oh, Daad!'

Our Genie

His parents named him Ala ad Din before they died, poor things. A bit of a misnomer that, since it means the glory of religion and the boy's about as religious as my floor mop, though nothing like as useful. Oh, you can't help liking him. I know I'm biased, as I'm his gran and I brought him up, but he's very lovable. He's got a sweet smile and a nice nature, too — apart from being bone idle. Good looking lad too; dark hair, dark eyes, flashing white teeth, slim build, nice muscles and all that. Takes after me. Well, in my young days, of course.

Our Aladdin does the odd day's work here and there, but it never lasts. He's got his head in the clouds, dreaming of all the wonderful opportunities that he thinks are going to be handed to him one day, like a dish of figs.

Gullible, the lad is. It's no wonder he was fooled by the wicked magician. I didn't like the look of that man from the start; all twirling black moustaches and smarmy charm he was. He claimed to be Aladdin's uncle, his father's long lost brother. There wasn't much resemblance, I can tell you that. He was a useless article, Aladdin's dad, not nearly good enough for my daughter, but there was nothing evil about him.

'Don't let him fool you,' I said to our Aladdin. But you can't tell them, can you? He was off to make his fortune courtesy of Mr. Smarmy Charm.

Actually, he did make his fortune, as it turned out.

That nasty bit of work lowered our Aladdin into a pit, with orders to find a valuable lamp that was down there. Luckily, he lent Aladdin a magic ring to help with the job. Aladdin was told that he just had to give the thing a good rub, and something would pop up. Same old story, eh?

Well, anyway, Aladdin tried it and, sure enough, a genie materialised. 'Your wish is my command, oh master,' style of thing.

The genie was so pleased to be free that it shot off to find the lamp, practically wagging its tail.

Next thing is that the wicked magician wanted Aladdin to throw up the lamp and the ring and then he'd pull him up out of the pit. Well, Aladdin, being a bit on the dim side, was just about to do it when the genie coughed a bit and whistled thoughtfully.

So Aladdin changed his mind. 'Pull me up first and give me my reward, then I'll hand over your lamp.'

There was a bit of an impasse for a while. Then the magician lost his rag and threw down the rope on top of Aladdin. 'Then stay there and die, insolent dog!'

Well Aladdin still had the ring and the genie.

The genie had to prompt him a bit, but he got the idea eventually.

'Take me home, genie.'

'Your wish is my command, oh master,' etc., and next minute they materialised right in the middle of our little courtyard, knocking over the dustbin.

I was a bit doubtful at first, but I quite took to that genie.

'Greetings, oh venerable lady,' he said when he saw me.

'Not so much of the venerable, thank you very much.'

'Greetings, oh beauteous one,' he amended, very smoothly, I thought.

'That's better, lad. Keep it coming,' I told him.

He definitely grinned at me. It's a rare thing, a genie with a sense of humour that doesn't involve pulling humans' arms and legs off. Your average genie I wouldn't give houseroom to, nasty homicidal things, but this one was quite user-friendly. A genial genie, you might say.

I found it came quite easily to me, commanding the genie. He was a dab hand with the housework before long. Even so, I was the one who discovered the secret of that lamp, while I was giving the manky thing a bit of a rub-up with some Brasso. Whoosh! This other genie appeared in a puff of dirty grey smoke — not what you want when you've just dusted.

This one was a big bugger.

'I am the Genie of the Lamp,' it announced, hovering over me with its arms crossed and a supercilious look on its ugly face. It didn't actually say 'Cower mortal scum,' but the thought was there. The Genie of the Ring took one look and whipped back inside like there was a snake after him. Can't say I blamed him.

'Here, Aladdin,' I called. 'You'd better come and sort this out.'

It all went to Aladdin's head, if you ask me. This new genie was a powerful one. The Genie of the Ring had conjured up a nice little three-bedroomed bungalow at the seaside for us, but with this new genie it was all palaces and servants and riches beyond the dreams of avarice.

I warned Aladdin. No-one can say I didn't.

'Be satisfied with what you've got,' I told him. 'If it's not broken don't mend it. We should stick with the Genie of the Ring. We're doing very nicely with him.'

Aladdin wouldn't listen. You know what lads are. He wanted the bigger, more powerful model.

'Size doesn't matter,' I told him, but I was wasting my breath.

Next thing you know Aladdin wants a princess to marry, if you please.

The Genie of the Lamp slipped up a bit with that princess mind you. She was a foreign one, Chinese or something. Princess Tai Chi, she was called. It didn't really matter. She and Aladdin seemed to speak the language of love. They spent most of the time gazing into each other's eyes. After all, conversation often comes later in the marriage, when the first flush has worn off, so to speak. Pretty girl, not very tall, but got all the right things in the right places, if you know what I mean. Aladdin kept saying how hot she was, though I don't know why she would be; she didn't wear many clothes. Very revealing, most of her stuff was. Anyway, she was a nice girl. Always respectful to her elders, me I mean, bowing to me and that, despite the fact she's a princess.

There was one serious problem with the language barrier. She didn't understand about the lamp. It so happened that I was at the market and Aladdin was off somewhere throwing his money around and impressing people, when this travelling lamp salesman came to the door. No prizes for guessing who that was.

'Special offer today,' Mr. Smarmy Charm says. 'New lamps for old, at no extra cost to the housewife.'

So, naturally, she brings out our battered old lamp and swaps it for a nice new one. As you would.

Well, a few minutes later the palace disappears in a puff of smoke. It wouldn't have bothered me, I was quite happy with my bungalow, but the trouble was that the princess vanished with the palace. Poor Aladdin was distraught. Well, I was upset myself. You can't let evil magicians go kidnapping innocent young girls. What with Aladdin moaning and wailing, I was in such a state I didn't know if I was coming or going. My mind was like one of those spiral staircases, going round and round and round, making me dizzy and a big drop either side if we got the plan of action wrong.

'Call up the Genie of the Ring,' I said to Aladdin.

'It's no good. He's not as powerful as the Genie of the Lamp,' Aladdin wailed.

'Well, at least he's on our side.'

The Genie of the Ring materialised looking a bit smug.

'I was expecting your call once everything went pear-shaped,' he said.

Well, that's a loose translation. There were a few more frills in the way he put it, obviously.

'Wow!' I said. I couldn't help myself. The genie was twice the man – supernatural demon thing – he had been before. He hovered in front of us, all gleaming oiled chest muscles and rippling biceps.

'I knew that bastard would give you grief, oh noble master and oh pearl of pulchritude' he told us. 'I've been working out.'

'And very nice too. But the evil magician won't be a pushover,' I warned him.

The genie braced himself and stretched, flexing

his pecs and grunting a bit, and suddenly there were two more huge, muscular arms, bristling with claws, springing from his magnificent chest.

'Forewarned is four-armed,' he said with aplomb.

For a moment he posed heroically, and then he reached out and gripped Aladdin with a friendly claw.

'Hi-ho human. Away!' he cried and they vanished to the rescue.

I'd have liked to go with them. I expect I'd just be in their way, though.

It's the waiting that's the worst when there's nothing you can do to help. Oh well, I suppose I could look out the first-aid kit and put the kettle on. They'll probably need a strong cuppa when they get home.

Chicken Licken

Henny Penny was dusting her little red henhouse. She had just opened the door to shake her feathers outside when she heard the screaming. Two youngsters came rushing down the road, squawking at the tops of their voices. The noise came nearer and nearer, like a reverse Doppler Effect, and she began to feel quite strange. Her heart thumped alarmingly and there was a buzzing in her ears. If she wasn't careful she'd have one of her turns and have to go and lie down. She was getting too old to cope with shocks. They made her go all dithery.

'Whatever's the matter?' she cried, hovering on the doorstep.

Her niece, Chicken Licken, rushed sobbing towards her and seized her by one wing. 'Oh Auntie Henny Penny, something terrible has happened. The sky is falling. A huge rock came out of nowhere and almost squashed me. Look!' She showed the crushed feathers on one wing.

'How could it happen?' gasped Henny Penny. Her beak hung open as she gazed in alarm at the frightened pair.

'It was an asteroid. The world is coming to an end!' cried young Ducky Lucky. 'It's all true. I've read about it online. Everyone is twittering about it. The ancient Mayan calendar predicts the end of the world this year and its predictions are never, never wrong. All the webbed-sites say the same.'

'Ooh!' Henny Penny clutched at her chest in shock. Everything inside her went cold and still. She didn't have a computer herself but she knew they were full of important information. 'Are you quite sure?'

'Today is December 21st, the day predicted to be the end of the world,' wailed Chicken Licken, 'and the sky is already beginning to fall. It's all coming true.'

By now Henny Penny's neighbours were flocking out into the street, anxious to find out what was happening. She felt relieved to see Drakey Lakey, who lived in one of the smarter houses, three doors down. He was such a clever, business-like duck, and doing very well for himself in the city. The others were inclined to be a bit flighty, but if anyone could understand all this, it would be Drakey Lakey. He stood high in the pecking order.

'What do you think Drakey Lakey?' she cried.

'Well now, I have read all about this in Chikipedia,' Drakey Lakey informed her, peering earnestly through the spectacles perched on his bill. 'It is the Mesoamerican Long Count Calendar to which they are referring.' He cleared his throat and spread his wings, ready to continue his informative lecture. 'The Mayans used calendar computations in a mathematical cycle, you see, and when the cycle has run its course a new cycle begins. The world is going to enter a new phase this year and it will lead to solar flares and earthquakes and all kinds of manifestations. I read on another webbed-site that this winter solstice the earth will be aligned with the centre of the Milky Way for the first time in 26,000 years.

'Ooh,' said Henny Penny weakly. All these numbers were making her head spin. Numbers couldn't lie, could they?

'It's all coming true!' shrieked Ducky Lucky, flapping distractedly.

'This is the dawning of the Age of Aquarius, the Age of Aquarius!' chanted another neighbour, Goosey Lucy, who tended to be a bit fey. She was much the same age as Henny Penny, but still wore her dishevelled feathers dyed red, with a brightly coloured band around her head. Goosey Lucy had been the first one in the barnyard to burn her boa and fly off the Greenham Common, back in the day.

Henny Penny gave her a flustered look. It didn't sound like anything to celebrate to her. She didn't think much of this 'Age of Aquarius' if it meant earthquakes and floods, and things falling out of the sky onto innocent young chicks. She felt thankful that she was no longer of an age to have eggs hatching. It was a dangerous, uncertain world. People who knew difficult scientific words were talking about things she didn't really understand, but there must be some truth in it if so many people believed it. Surely somebody ought to take charge and report the catastrophe to the proper authorities.

'We should go and tell them at the town hall,' she clucked. 'The authorities will know what to do.' She had great faith in the government. Such clever people were bound to be able to solve the problem.

'I heartily agree,' said Drakey Lakey, puffing out his chest feathers. 'And I will volunteer to be the spokesbird when we arrive. I'm sure the authorities will listen to me.'

Drakey Lakey, now appointed leader of the flock, set off, with the others flapping along behind him. Henny Penny was determined to keep up with the youngsters. The cobbled street was hard on her poor claws but she hurried along as best she could, keen to do her civic duty.

Further down the street they met Turkey Lurkey and Cocky Locky, hanging about on the corner, trying to look cool. They were eyeing up the talent, as they called it, which meant annoying any female who walked by. It would be those two, just when someone sensible was needed, Henny Penny thought. Still anyone was better than no-one today.

'Oh Turkey Lurkey, have you heard that the sky is falling and the world is coming to an end? It's on all the webbed-sites online,' Henny Penny cried.

Turkey Lurkey eyed her with respect. 'Hey, you is one cool chick. I never knowed that you is a silver surfer. Yeah, I hears de buzz. Dere's gonna to be a collish-un wid an asteroid right, or a planet, or maybe some big deal solar bang? Kerpowee!'

Henny Penny had no idea why he was talking like that. She knew his old mother, born and bred in Scunthorpe. Still he seemed to have the right idea.

'Will you come with us to find help?' She cried.

Turkey Lurkey and Cocky Locky high-fived each other with their wings. 'We's with yuh, dude!'

They hurried along the verge beside the road into town. Traffic roared past them. Henny Penny felt the ground vibrate beneath her. Probably an earthquake starting, she thought nervously. It was all the fault of those Mayans. The others seemed to think so too. Ducky Lucky gave a little scream and Chicken Licken clutched at her auntie's wing.

As they passed a ruined wartime bunker at the edge of town, Drakey Lakey stopped, abruptly. He took off his glasses, cleaned them on his breast feathers, then put them back on and stretched out a wing to point. 'Look there, a place that could have been made for us, in our hour of need. A bunker, to help us survive the catastrophe to come. We must gather food, so when civilisation comes to an end we are prepared,' he pronounced. 'They say that only a few meals stand between birdkind and savagery. Birds of a feather must flock together for protection. We must stiffen our sinews, summon up the blood, disguise fair nature with hard-favour'd rage...'

103

'Fight off any gangsta dat tries moving in on our turf,' cried Turkey Lurkey.

'Yeah, bro, dat's our bunker!' shouted Cocky Locky strutting aggressively.

'Fight them on the beaches,' thought Henny Penny distractedly. She wasn't sure she could manage savagery. She supposed she could try, if she really had to.

It seemed, however, that the bunker was not as empty as they had thought. As they stood there, a large, red gold shape came slinking out of the doorway and stood staring at them in surprise.

Foxy Loxy.

'Ooh, Foxy Loxy, are you going to survive the destruction in that bunker?' cried Chicken Licken excitedly. 'Have you stocked it with food ready?'

'Not yet,' Foxy Loxy replied courteously. 'Now tell me, friends, what is this destruction you're so worried about?'

'The sky is falling on our heads,' cried Chicken Licken.

A babble of voices broke out, telling him that it was the end of the world, and that the Mayan prophesies were all coming true.

'We were on our way to the town hall to report this phenomenon and demand that action is taken when we saw this bunker,' added Drakey Lakey. 'We were unaware that you had a prior claim.'

Foxy Loxy prowled towards them and for a

moment Henny Penny felt a little nervous. He was smiling welcomingly but his teeth seemed very white and strong. For a moment he looked rather…well, vulpine. However, he only raised his front paws calmingly over the frightened poultry.

'Come in brothers and sisters, and be welcome. If my bunker can provide any protection from the doom that is upon us, then I will gladly share it with my flock. Now, calm yourselves,' he murmured soothingly. 'For all the creatures of earth are as one under the heavens.' He raised his eyes devoutly. 'If the end is coming then we must forget the cares of this transitory life and prepare our souls for the next world. Sister, if I may?' With one paw, he lifted the bird-with-outstretched-wings symbol hanging on a silver chain around Goosey Lucy's neck and arranged it carefully around his own. It was clearly a significant gesture, but Henny Penny was not quite sure what it actually did signify. At least the bird was not oven-ready, she thought, which was reassuring.

Inside the ruined bunker all was quiet and peaceful, and the light was dim. Henny Penny perched herself gratefully on a broken wooden seat. Now that she felt safer, she knew she needed to rest and recover. This was all too much for a geriatric old bird. She struggled with her tiredness, but she could feel her eyelids drooping. She could barely stay awake.

In the background she heard the mellifluous voice of Foxy Loxy speaking again. 'We must pray together brothers and sisters,' he said. 'For behold, all this is prophesied. It is the time of the seventh seal, which, when broken, shall bring plague and earthquake, hail, fire, famine and drought and meteor strike.'

'Seals,' thought Henny Penny half asleep. Poor little things, they'd all die in a meteor strike.

She was dimly aware of Foxy Loxy's eyes. They were beautiful; soft and brown and glowing with love and they seemed to be looking at her alone, singling her out for his care. It was difficult to look away. She wondered if the others felt the same and saw that they too were gazing enraptured into those wonderful, hypnotic eyes.

'It is judgement day, my feathered friends, Armageddon, the Apocalypse,' cried the charismatic Foxy Loxy. 'Woe upon us all'. He cast his paws up to heaven.

'Woe, woe,' cried his congregation rocking in time with his waving paws.

'Whoa,' clucked Henny Penny vaguely.

'I have had a revelation!' cried Foxy Loxy. 'A great mountain of fire shall be cast into the sea and the sun shall darken. It is time, brothers and sisters. The earth must be destroyed!'

'What shall we do?' wailed Chicken Licken, gazing at him like one transfixed.

'Guru, help us, save us,' cried Ducky Lucky hysterically.

'Alleluia!' cried Foxy Loxy.

'Alleluia!' echoed his flock.

Through half closed eyes, Henny Penny could see shadows dancing in the dimness of the bunker. All her friends were swaying rhythmically to Foxy Loxy's voice. Even Drakey Lakey was clapping happily with the rest of the flock. Goosey Lucy was chanting a mantra and dancing a little dance to herself, her eyes glazed with the spirit that had come upon her. Turkey Lurkey and Cocky Locky were throwing up their wings in ecstasy and squawking in tongues. Henny Penny struggled with her terrible drowsiness. It was intoxicating. She wanted to be a part of this glorious moment. If only she could stay awake.

'Do not despair, my children,' cried Foxy Loxy. 'Your bodies must perish, but behold, in the wake of the comet of destruction comes the vessel of the masters of the universe, which shall bear away your souls to paradise. Gather round, brothers and sisters, death is but a gateway to salvation for you. For you are the Chosen Ones.'

Henny Penny was dimly aware of Chicken Licken, Ducky Lucky, Drakey Lakey, Goosey Lucy, Turkey Lurkey and Cocky Locky following in procession behind Foxy Loxy, swaying and chanting, never taking their eyes from him.

'Brothers and sisters,' he barked. 'I shall now pray for you all'.

Henny Penny was sure that was what he said,

but it sounded oddly like, 'Prey on you all.'

Moments later, when she struggled back from the depths of her old age nap, the bunker was empty except for a few feathers.

'Where has everyone gone?' she clucked, flapping anxiously around the empty room.

The sharp nose of Foxy Loxy poked round the door of the bunker. He smiled again, showing those beautiful white teeth, and his glowing eyes fixed hypnotically on her.

'The Rapture has taken them, sister,' he said, licking his lips.

Lightning Source UK Ltd.
Milton Keynes UK
UKHW01f0736120918
328757UK00003B/11/P